# Goddess

# Goddess

*A Child of the Sixties*

## Ginny Brinkley

Copyright © 2018 by Ginny Brinkley.

| | | |
|---|---|---|
| Library of Congress Control Number: | | 2018911491 |
| ISBN: | Hardcover | 978-1-9845-5569-4 |
| | Softcover | 978-1-9845-5570-0 |
| | eBook | 978-1-9845-5571-7 |

All rights reserved. No part of this book may be reproduced or transmitted in any form or by any means, electronic or mechanical, including photocopying, recording, or by any information storage and retrieval system, without permission in writing from the copyright owner.

This tale is fiction. Any similarities to persons living or deceased is purely coincidental. Some of the events, however, were inspired by incidents that took place at Mary Washington College of the University of Virginia in the 1960s.

Print information available on the last page.

Rev. date: 09/27/2018

**To order additional copies of this book, contact:**
Xlibris
1-888-795-4274
www.Xlibris.com
Orders@Xlibris.com
775766

# CONTENTS

Chapter 1 "Yesterday's Gone" ..................................................................1
Chapter 2 "Then He Kissed Me" ..............................................................5
Chapter 3 "Young Love" ...........................................................................9
Chapter 4 "Summertime Blues" .............................................................14
Chapter 5 "Starry, Starry Night" ............................................................19
Chapter 6 "Be True to Your School" ......................................................25
Chapter 7 "With a Little Help from My Friends" ................................31
Chapter 8 "Back in My Arms Again" ....................................................34
Chapter 9 "I Will Survive" ......................................................................39
Chapter 10 "P.S. I Love You" ..................................................................43
Chapter 11 "Only the Lonely" ................................................................45
Chapter 12 "Heat Wave" .........................................................................49
Chapter 13 "Nothing but Heartaches" ..................................................53
Chapter 14 "School Days" .......................................................................57
Chapter 15 "Hit the Road Jack" .............................................................62
Chapter 16 "Please Mr. Postman" ..........................................................67
Chapter 17 "In the Midnight Hour" ......................................................72
Chapter 18 "Tragedy" ..............................................................................75
Chapter 19 "Apples, Peaches, Pumpkin Pie" ........................................77
Chapter 20 "You've Got a Friend" .........................................................82
Chapter 21 "Home for the Holidays" ....................................................85
Chapter 22 "Blue Velvet" .........................................................................89
Chapter 23 "A Hazy Shade of Winter" ..................................................92
Chapter 24 "Save the Last Dance for Me" ............................................97
Chapter 25 "Did You Ever Have to Make Up Your Mind?" ......... 102
Chapter 26 "You Don't Have to Say You Love Me" ....................... 107
Chapter 27 "Graduation Day" ............................................................ 111

| | | |
|---|---|---|
| Chapter 28 | "I Can See Clearly Now" | 115 |
| Chapter 29 | "Going to the Chapel" | 121 |
| Chapter 30 | "With This Ring" | 125 |
| Chapter 31 | "It's Only Make Believe" | 130 |
| Chapter 32 | "To the Aisle" | 134 |
| Chapter 33 | "Baby Love" | 138 |
| Chapter 34 | "Second Honeymoon" | 141 |
| Chapter 35 | "Do You Believe in Magic?" | 145 |
| Chapter 36 | "Dream a Little Dream of Me" | 148 |
| Chapter 37 | "The Sounds of Silence" | 151 |
| Chapter 38 | "A Teenager in Love" | 153 |
| Chapter 39 | "Sixteen Candles" | 156 |
| Chapter 40 | "Midnight Confessions" | 161 |
| Chapter 41 | "Turn! Turn! Turn! (To Everything There Is a Season)" | 165 |
| Chapter 42 | "Searchin'" | 170 |
| Chapter 43 | "Manic Monday" | 173 |
| Chapter 44 | In the Cabin "Girl Talk" | 177 |
| Chapter 45 | "Reach Out I'll Be There" | 182 |
| Chapter 46 | "The Answer Is Blowing in the Wind" | 185 |
| Chapter 47 | "The Long and Winding Road" | 189 |
| Chapter 48 | "If I Could Turn Back Time" | 196 |

To everyone who's ever had a first love.

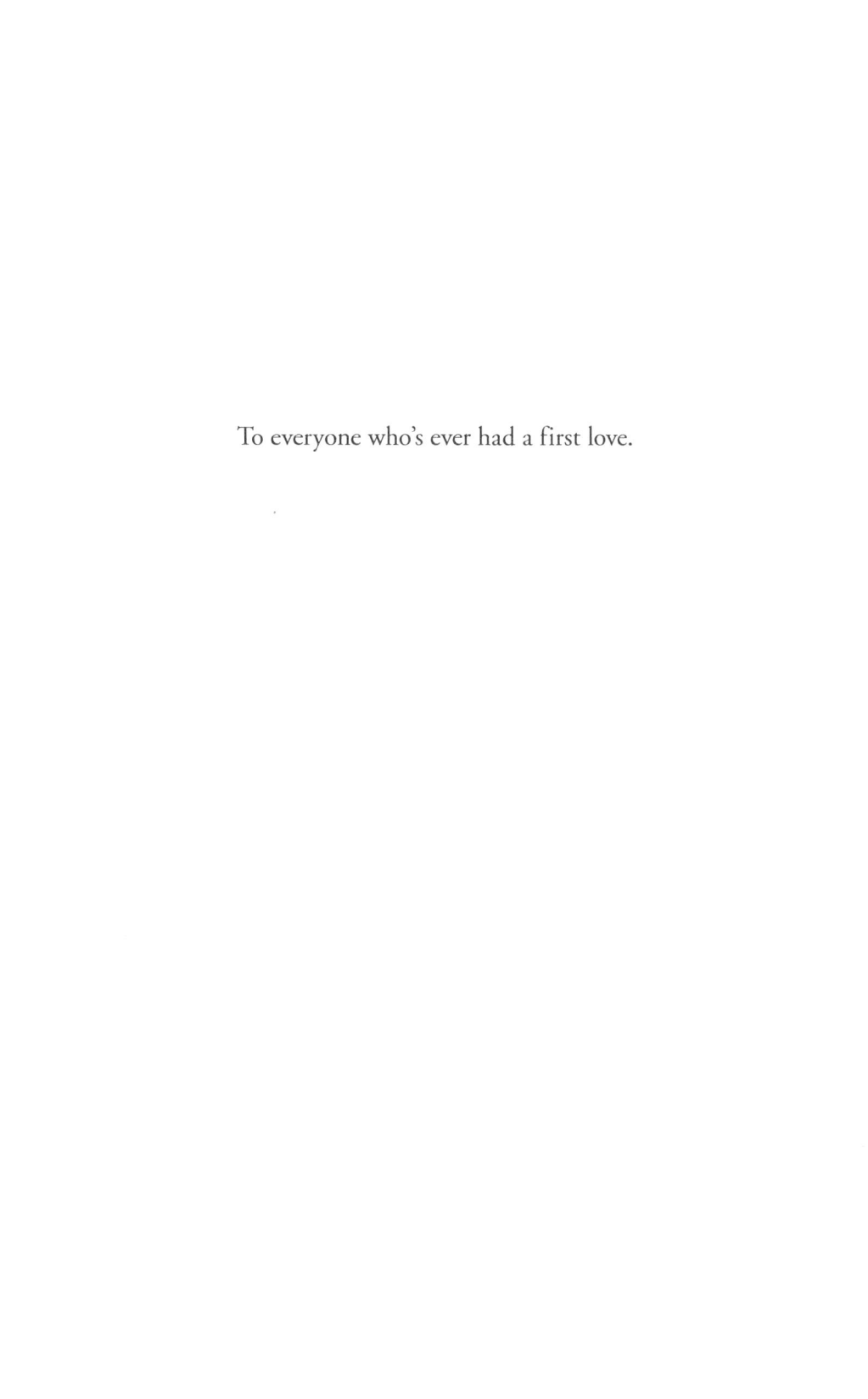

Goddesshood resides in every woman.

Cherish those who honor your inner goddess.

# ACKNOWLEDGMENTS

A handful of amazing people assisted in the creation of this work. My designated readers were invaluable in keeping the story on point, credible, and coherent. Many thanks to Renee Faure, Nana Royer, Ryan Davis, Samantha Ryan, Kelli Conley, Jane Bryant, Maryanne Hewitt, Ashton Garcia, and the late Anne Riggins.

I am deeply grateful to Summer Morris for once again working her magic on the cover and to the lovely Kelli Conley for sharing her modeling talents.

Much appreciation to Dave Perkins for providing his computer expertise, and most importantly, to my loving husband, Bill, for his endless patience and support.

# 2011

## CHAPTER 1

## "Yesterday's Gone"[1]

"Summer storms are always the worst," Annie announced to her four-legged companion as the two of them hurried up the muddy path to the cabin, hoping to dodge the raindrops and avoid any lightning bolts. Tulip scooted ahead and raced to the door while Annie sloshed along behind, fumbling in her purse for the key. Just as she got to the door, her cell phone began playing a familiar tune. She knew she wanted to take this call and grabbed the phone, dropping her keys in the puddle at her feet.

"Hi, Ringo!" she exclaimed into the phone.

"Hi, Roomie," the voice responded. "How are you?"

"I'm a little wet," Annie replied. "Tulip and I are just arriving at the cabin, and it's storming," she explained, retrieving her keys and struggling to unlock the door. Before it was fully open, Tulip began barking furiously, then pushed her way in and headed toward the kitchen, leaving a trail of wet leaves in her wake.

"Ringo, I'll have to call you back. Tulip's having a fit! She's after something, and I've got to find out what it is!" Annie shouted.

"NO! WAIT! Maybe I should stay on the line!" Ringo said and then added, "I hope it's not ghosts."

---

1. "Yesterday's Gone"; artist: Chad & Jeremy; released 1964.

Any other time, Annie might have found Ringo's comment amusing but not now.

"Not funny! I'll call you back." Clicking off, she hurried to the kitchen, her heart pounding. Annie found her beloved yellow lab in front of the pantry door, still barking madly. She looked around for the nearest weapon and grabbed a frying pan, then slowly pushed open the pantry door.

Gagging at the stench, she saw what appeared to be dried blood spattered on the floor. The stain was coming out from under the bottom shelf in the pantry. Covering her nose and getting down on the floor to peer under the shelf, she discovered the partially decomposed body of a rat, mangled by a rusty rodent trap.

"No, Tulip, stay back!" she yelled, relieved, though somewhat sickened, by her find. "I guess we can thank your daddy for this," she continued to the dog, who obviously found the smell way more enticing than she did. "He was so insistent on setting these traps. I would have preferred just shooing the poor critters outside and letting them live. I hope his ghost *is* here so he can witness the mess he created. Now I've got to clean it up before unpacking the car. I wonder how long this thing has been here."

Knowing Ringo would be worried about her, she took a minute to send her a quick message before tackling the job at hand. She texted,

> *"All's fine here, just a dead rat! Will call you in a bit after we settle in and get this place cleaned up."*

This was Annie's first visit to the cabin by herself, so perhaps the unplanned dead-rat incident had been a good distraction, she mused later, after thoroughly scrubbing and disinfecting the pantry and unloading the car. It had certainly kept her from dwelling on her aloneness. It wasn't that Annie minded being alone; she'd had two years to get used to that. It was the being alone *here* that was so hard.

"Thank goodness I have you with me," she said to the loyal pup at her feet, who had finally given up on the possibility of rat stew for lunch and had settled down on the kitchen floor, awaiting the next adventure.

"We've been through so much together, us old gals. I know you must miss him too," Annie continued to the oblivious pooch.

Annie made herself a cup of tea and sat down at the kitchen table to ponder her situation. *This was always our place,* she thought, *our secret haven, so ideally situated at the edge of the beautiful Blue Ridge Mountains. We both loved it here so much, planning for it all those years, then bringing it to fruition. Our place. For fifteen years. Now what am I to do?* She almost felt guilty being there without him.

*But I'm here with a purpose,* she continued in her mind. Was it too late to look for happiness again? More importantly, did she even *deserve* happiness after all that had happened? Why had she been brought to this point in her life? Where was she to go from here? So many unanswered questions.

She thought back to what her sweet Grammy used to tell her when she was growing up, "If you follow your inner feelings, you'll always know the right choices when they come along. You just need to take the time to get in touch with those feelings." *Such simple advice,* she mused. *Not quite so simple to carry out.* Over the years, Annie had developed her own version of her Gram's advice, that if you are in tune with the Universe, your higher self will know the right choices.

"That is why I'm up here now," she said out loud to anyone who might be listening, "to get in touch with my higher self and figure out those inner feelings." Tulip ignored her.

Although her dear grandmother had been gone for many years, her influence during Annie's early years had been so profound that Annie still felt her presence at times like this. "Grammy, if you're out there, I sure could use some help right now," she called out in a loud voice, just to make sure her Gram's spirit would hear her. This startled Tulip, who immediately jumped up, looking for whoever might be coming. "Oh sorry, Tulip," Annie apologized to the dog. "It's okay. No one's coming."

Annie poured another cup of tea, sat down again, and took a deep breath. *How did it all happen anyway?* she asked herself. Her mind took her back to her high school days and the memory of those first youthful yearnings nearly fifty years in the past.

She closed her eyes. *Her thoughts went immediately to her first love. Sometimes it seems like just last week. Ned and I were best buddies back then. Neither of us had many other friends, so if we went anywhere, it was usually with each other. Inevitably, we discovered sex together too. Sitting in his car on a warm summer evening, we'd fumble our way along, almost innocently, led by our youthful urges, yet not knowing what to do with them. I remember kissing for so long that our lips would be sore and swollen for hours afterwards. And the groping—his hands, nervously exploring my body, causing that electrifying sensation wherever he made contact on my bare skin. Oh, to experience that type of arousal again! I wonder if it's still possible . . .*

"We better get comfortable, sweet girl," Annie said to Tulip. "I'll be taking a little trip down memory lane. It's going to be a long afternoon." She got out a legal pad and picked up her pen.

# 1961

## CHAPTER 2

## "Then He Kissed Me"[2]

I'm not exactly sure when we first laid eyes on each other, but I'm pretty certain that the first time we actually spoke was at the beginning of my senior year of high school, in physics class. Being nearsighted, I always chose a seat in the front of the classroom so I could see the board. In physics, we had three rows of tables with two students sitting at each table. I had picked the table in the middle row and closest to the front, directly opposite the teacher's desk. Ned was even more introverted than I was, so I never could figure out why he chose to sit at my table in the front of the room. He later claimed that it was because of me, but I think probably the truth was that it was the only seat left when he came in. Maybe it was fate.

As Ned sat down that first day, he tossed a quick hi in my direction, along with a hint of a grin, his sandy hair falling loosely on his forehead. His obvious shyness caught me off guard, and the sweetness behind his crooked smile melted something inside me. I stuttered back some clever reply like "Hi, yourself." Then I spent the rest of the class period thinking of all the responses that I could have come up with that would have been more impressive.

Because we were now "lab partners," Ned and I were forced to communicate on occasion with such meaningful comments as "What

---

2. "Then He Kissed Me"; artist: The Crystals; released 1963.

does she mean by number 7?" Even then, I could detect a bit of humor underneath his words, and I was eager to dig beneath this quiet exterior and get to know him better. My most significant early memories of "us" were when Ned would ask me to pass him something, like the ruler or protractor. He always managed to touch my hand, very briefly, while taking it from me. That's when I first noticed the electricity. It was overwhelming I almost couldn't stand it. Was he feeling it too? It was so overpowering I thought that maybe sparks were flying between us and that the whole class could see them! I'd desperately try to keep myself composed and act perfectly normal whenever that happened, not letting on that my panties were getting soggier by the second.

The other thing was the twinkle in his eyes. I'd never totally understood before what a "twinkle" was. But there was no mistaking this. It was a definite twinkle, and there was no other word for it. I first remember being aware of it when I gathered my courage and suggested that we study for an upcoming test together. I was trying to sound casual.

"I'm not clear on that last chapter. Would you have time after school this afternoon to go over it with me?" I asked, looking directly into those green eyes and holding my breath.

He hesitated briefly, gave me that crazy half grin, along with the eye twinkle, and replied, "Now, Annie, what do you really have in mind? Can I trust you outside the classroom?"

Ah, saved by the humor. "Well, I don't know. I guess there's only one way to find out." So that's how our first date came about, on a Thursday afternoon, in his '57 Chevy. We went for root beer. We talked mostly about our families, our pets, and where we'd been. He didn't touch me. And we never got around to discussing physics. I got an A on the test. He got a B.

It wasn't until after Thanksgiving that we had a real date, where he actually came to my house and met my parents. I could tell he was really nervous about meeting them, so we got out of there as quickly as we could. We went to an early showing of *West Side Story*, then to a drive-in restaurant for root beer. He kept teasing me about how I was just using him to get better grades in physics.

We'd been laughing all evening, but when we got back to my house and he stopped the car, things got awkward. It was too quiet sitting there in the car in the dark. We made small talk.

"Good movie."

"Yeah."

"Nice evening."

"Yeah."

I realized he was getting up his nerve.

"I want to kiss you, Annie."

Before I could think of a response, he continued. "I've never kissed a girl before. I'm not sure what to do."

"You just do it," I blurted out, noticing that my body was already reacting in anticipation of what was to come, and wishing that he'd hurry up and get on with it.

"But where do I put my hands?"

"You just put them wherever feels right." I was beginning to get impatient and afraid that he wasn't ever going to do it. I mean, I'd heard of guys who were naive and inexperienced, but some things just come naturally, don't they? I didn't know how much longer I could wait without exploding.

That's when his lips touched mine, very gently, causing shivers over my whole body. I put my arms around his shoulders and pulled him closer. I did not want the moment to end. I could see why people kill for this sensation. I tried to memorize exactly how it felt so I could re-enact it in my dreams. "Please don't stop," I pleaded silently. "Make this feeling last forever."

He slowly pulled away. "Wow. That was good," he said, smiling and acting like a kid who had discovered ice cream for the first time. "Let's do it again."

We entwined again, and I dissolved into him. When he pulled away this time, I took his hand and held it in both of mine. I didn't want the touching to stop. We sat quietly for a minute, then he spoke.

"Annie, I'm really new at this, and I want to do it right. I don't even know what you're supposed to do between kisses."

I laughed. He really *was* that naive. "You just do what you're doing," I said. What I wanted was for him to kiss me again. And he did.

"I need to get you home now," he announced after a few more embraces. "Your parents will be coming out here to see what's going on. But I need to wait a few minutes before getting out of the car. Let's talk about the movie some more." I noticed that Paul Anka was singing "Puppy Love" on the car radio.

That night as I lay in bed, I replayed the entire evening over and over in my head. I didn't want to ever forget how it felt to be held that way, the anticipation and excitement. I finally dozed off into fitful dreams of Ned kissing me, the two of us on the verge of combustion.

# 1962

# CHAPTER 3

## "Young Love"[3]

As the school year progressed, so did our involvement. Every time we went out, we'd end up parking and kissing. Sometimes we'd even skip the movie and just go park. On each occasion, his hands would explore a little more of my body, and a new sensation was felt and memorized. I found that his innocence only served to enhance my excitement. Before he would touch me, he would ask if it was okay. Then he would proceed. Watching his obvious delight as he experienced the various parts of a female body for the first time was thrilling for me. The physical sensations just kept getting better and better.

At first, he noticeably avoided my breasts, being careful to work around them. He'd rub my shoulders and back, stroke my belly, touch my face, my hands, and sometimes even my feet. Then one night, while his hand was under my sweater gently caressing my midsection, he slowly began moving it towards my chest. An experienced lover could not have given me more of a thrill. I moaned softly as his fingers discovered my waiting nipples.

"Is this okay?" he whispered. My sounds of pleasure provided the answer.

He took my hand and placed it on the bulge in his pants, sending chills up my spine. I was surprised to find that he, too, was wet with

---

3. "Young Love"; artist: Sonny James; released 1957.

anticipation, evident even through his slacks. By now I was aching for release, and I knew he was too. There was no turning back.

"We can't do this," I said, suddenly realizing where this was headed.

"We won't do THAT," Ned replied gently. "But we can do other things. Just let me touch you there."

There? Down there? He was going to touch me *down there*? That is what our health and P.E. teachers had all warned us about, "Don't ever let a boy touch you *down there*." But I desperately wanted the excitement to continue, and he had assured me that he wouldn't do THAT.

"Okay," I said.

His hand slowly moved up my skirt, teasing my thighs as it found its way into my panties. The warmth of his fingers pressed against my wetness, and he began a gentle stroking. Before I knew what was happening, I exploded into orgasm.

"Oh, Annie, you came! You came! I love making you do that!" He started stroking again, and another wave of pleasure came over me. Now I was like putty in his hands, and he was like a kid with a new toy. He brought me to orgasm three or four more times and would have continued if I hadn't convinced him that I was exhausted and a little sore.

"Don't you want to try for twenty-five?" he asked, making me laugh.

Right after that, he took me home. "What about you?" I asked. "Are you okay?" I was feeling guilty that he had given me so much pleasure and I had given him none.

"I'm fine," he replied. "My enjoyment is in satisfying you." I knew then that he was stealing my heart. And I was pretty certain that it was mutual.

The school year would be ending soon, with graduation coming up in June. We talked about our summer plans, pledging to spend much time together. Everything was great for us then. We were falling in love, we were hot for each other, we had the whole summer ahead of us, and he continued to make me laugh.

The next time we went out, we first went to a movie but left before it was over. Ned's car was becoming our favorite place. I was anxious to feel his touch again. We quickly drove to our usual parking spot and began kissing. He proceeded slowly from there, driving me crazy. This time he unzipped his pants before placing my hand on him. His penis seemed huge to me, as he guided my hand along the shaft.

"You need to milk it like this," he explained, showing me how to lubricate the end. After a few tries, I caught on to what he wanted, and he leaned back to enjoy it. In a minute, he took some tissues and held them in his lap.

"It's coming now," he announced almost matter-of-factly. He stiffened, moaning. "Oh god!" he exclaimed as his body convulsed. Then he relaxed and immediately handed me another tissue to wipe my hand. He was quiet for a moment.

"I think I'm in love with you, Annie."

"I know," I said. "I love you too." We held each other for a long time.

On another memorable Saturday evening, we ventured into nearby Fairfax County to a drive-in theater to see *Splendor in the Grass*, the story of Bud and Deanie, two young lovers whose intense passion for each other was so much like our own. We sat intertwined throughout the movie, captivated by the tale unfolding on the big screen. For that brief time, Ned *was* Warren Beatty, and I *was* Natalie Wood, as we experienced Bud's and Deanie's emotions, longings, and struggles as if they were our own. We were, however, envisioning a more favorable outcome for the two of us than the one they were handed.

Things seemed nearly perfect. We spent most weekends together. We talked, we laughed, we kissed, we shared an intimacy I didn't know was possible. And he never pressured me to go further sexually than I felt comfortable with. As long as we could stimulate each other manually, he didn't push me to have intercourse. Technically, we both remained virgins all the way through high school.

Our only problem was Ned's mother. She apparently felt that her "little boy" was getting too serious too soon. Ned didn't actually tell me this at first, probably thinking that she would get over it. It took me a while to discern what was going on. She even invited me over for dinner a few times, being quite hospitable on those occasions. My first clue of any difficulty was that whenever I called their house and she answered, it seemed that Ned wasn't home or wasn't "available." Sometimes he would pick up on another phone, saying, "I'm here, Mom." Often, when I left a message with her for him to call, he would call me very soon anyway, and I would just assume that it was in response to my call. I found out later that he seldom received my messages.

One evening, a few days before our high school graduation, he brought up the topic of his mother.

"I wonder why she's so against me," I pondered, half questioning to see if he had an explanation.

"She's afraid we're going to get married," he responded immediately.

"Why would she think that?" I asked.

"Because she knows that's what I want to do."

"You do? Oh, I want that too, Ned, but not now. We need to go to college and all that first."

"I want to marry you now, Annie. I will always love only you. There's no reason to wait. If we get married after graduation, I can work and go to college at night. Other people do that; we could too. I just want to be with you all the time."

I didn't know what to say. We had never really discussed marriage before, except in a dreamy sort of way about some time in the future. I pictured us together in a house with a white picket fence and a couple of little Neds running around. But not yet. I was planning to go away to college. I wanted to live in a dorm and have the full "college experience." I wanted Ned to have it too.

"I think we're too young to get married," was all I said. "Your mother may be right."

He took me home early that night.

The next time the subject came up, Ned calmly announced that he thought he might put off college for a while. He was tired of "book work," he said, and he wanted to make some money. I didn't take his comments seriously, assuming that he was just having temporary doubts. He had always planned to attend college, and his parents had always planned for it too. So I didn't see any need to argue or react strongly. His parents were sure to do that.

"If you feel that's what you need to do, then do it," was all I said.

The day after our graduation, Ned and I had plans to go to the beach. He picked me up early, and we headed towards the coast, an almost three-hour drive from our little town of Fort Custis, Virginia, located just outside our nation's capital. I noticed that Ned was unusually quiet, obviously preoccupied with something. About halfway there, he suddenly pulled the car off the road and stopped.

"We have to talk, Annie."

"What is it?"

"I've made a decision. I'm going away for a while."

"Wha—"

He didn't let me speak. "I have a cousin in Colorado who works on a ranch. He says there's lots of work for anyone who wants it. It would be hard, but I've never been out West, and if I'm ever going to do it, now seems like the time." Then he was quiet.

"For how long?" was all I could get out, tears rolling down my cheeks.

"I don't know."

"What about us?" I asked, sobbing.

"Oh, Annie, I'll be back. I promise." He was holding me as I cried uncontrollably.

I knew I had to let him do it. Asking him not to go would be like attaching a ball and chain to him. I hated girls who did that to their boyfriends. I had to be brave and face the summer without him for his sake. I knew he loved me.

"Maybe it will be good for us," I blubbered, trying so hard to do the right thing. "You know, 'Absence makes the heart grow fonder.'"

"Yeah."

We never made it to the beach. After sitting in the car talking for several hours, we turned around and went home. Ned was leaving the next day and had packing to do.

I was in a state of shock. My world was crumbling.

# CHAPTER 4

## "Summertime Blues"[4]

I didn't know if I would survive the summer, but I was determined to try. My job as a file clerk with a local law firm occupied my days. The nights were not so easy. And the weekends were the worst. My dad found out about a photography club that met on Saturdays, and I was just desperate enough that I decided to join it. Taking pictures had been my hobby over the years, and I still had a decent camera.

On Sundays, I'd write long letters to Ned, telling him everything I'd done all week, often including some of my photos.

Ned's letters to me were short but wonderful. In each one, he declared his love, and I treasured them all, reading them over and over. He was able to call about once a week but could only talk briefly. Calling on a pay phone, he'd pay in advance to talk for three minutes. The message "Your three minutes are up, sir. Please deposit more coins," abruptly ended many of our conversations. Those brief calls were what I lived for. I loved hearing his voice.

Before leaving, Ned had told me that I was free to go out with other guys, but I assured him that I wouldn't want to. In mid-July, the law firm where I was working was having a party, and one of the law students interning there for the summer invited me to go with him. We had eaten lunch together a few times, during which I had talked

---

4. "Summertime Blues"; artist: Eddie Cochran; released 1958.

nonstop about Ned, so I figured he would be a safe date for the party. His name was Steve.

The party was held on what was probably the hottest day all summer at the home of one of the firm's partners, outside by the pool. As soon as we arrived, Steve located two cups of cold beer and handed me one. I had only had beer a few times and didn't like it much. This time, however, it was surprisingly refreshing, thanks, no doubt, to the extreme heat and humidity. It didn't take long for me to empty my cup, and Steve was right there with a refill. I remember one more refill, and there might have been another after that.

I don't remember much about the ride home, just some laughter. When we stopped at my house, Steve turned to me, pulled me close, and kissed me. I did not resist. I closed my eyes and tried to pretend it was Ned kissing me. But there was no electricity, not a single spark.

I awoke early the next morning with a headache. The phone was ringing. My mother answered it and appeared at my bedroom door.

"It's Ned," she said.

I grabbed the phone next to my bed. "Ned?"

"I saw you," he said in a tone I didn't understand.

"What?"

"I saw you. Last night. I saw you in the car. With that guy. Kissing."

"Ned, where are you?"

"I'm at home. I came home yesterday. I missed you so much. And I rushed over to see you, and there you were kissing someone else! Annie, how *could* you?"

"Ned, it's not what it seems. I love *you*. I pretended he was you. I had been drinking." My explanation seemed to be making things worse. I tried again.

"It wasn't anything. I swear. Please, Ned, come over. I want to see you."

"I can't right now, Annie. I'm too upset. I'll talk to you later."

He didn't call back. I couldn't stand it. I tried calling his house several times, but his mother answered and said he wasn't there. I finally borrowed my mom's car and drove to his house. His mother met me at the door. She said she didn't know where he'd gone, that she hadn't seen him for hours and that he'd appeared very upset when he left. I believed her. The garage was closed, so I couldn't tell if his car was there or not.

I drove around awhile, checking all our favorite places. No luck. I went back to his house and parked down the street and watched. Nothing. The feeling of emptiness I was experiencing was growing by the minute. Had I totally messed up my life with Ned by one stupid action? Had I lost him forever?

It was getting late. Reluctantly, I started the car and headed for home. There were no messages from Ned. I didn't know what else I could do. The next day was Monday, and I'd be at work all day. I tried calling his house two more times. His mother again. No word from him, she said. I began to wonder if he was okay.

Monday at work was the day from hell. I wasn't eating, hadn't slept, was worried sick over Ned, and I had to face my co-workers. Apparently, I had done some rather crazy things at the party. Several people asked if I was feeling better. Steve even made it a point to apologize for any trouble he had caused. He had no idea of the trouble he had caused. My life was ruined.

When I got home from work, Ned was there. He was sitting in the living room, talking to my mom. After I came in, she left us alone. I rushed to Ned, and he stood and embraced me.

"Oh, Ned, where have you been? I'm so sorry. I love you. I love you. I'll never go out with anyone else again. Please, please, please forgive me. I am so happy to see you." Then I paused to enjoy the moment. His touch was overwhelming, and as I became still, I could feel my nerve endings responding to his body, the electricity igniting in each fiber. How I'd missed that! But the joy quickly ended.

"Annie, I've joined the Army."

I gasped. "You're joking, right?"

"No, I'm serious."

"How? Why?"

"Because if I'm not going to college, I need to do something else meaningful, and since everything's changed between us now, I might as well see the world. I signed up this afternoon."

"What do you mean 'since everything's changed between us now'?"

"I *saw* you with that guy. I can't believe that was the only time you went out with him. You were *kissing*. And you'd been drinking! You never used to drink. I feel like I don't even know you anymore."

"I can explain all that. He was just a friend who works where I do, and he knows all about you. It was a company party, and it was hot outside, and the beer was cold, and I had too much. I had never done that before, and I certainly will never do it again."

Ned listened thoughtfully as I explained. Then he spoke again. "But what about yesterday? I was so hurt when we talked, I just had to hang up. If you wanted to see me so badly, why didn't you call me back?"

"What? I *did* call you. Several times. You weren't there. Then I went by your house. You still weren't there. Your mother didn't even know where you'd gone."

"My mother? Oh no. I was there all along. I fell asleep in the afternoon and must have slept a while. I was exhausted after being up all night thinking about us. I never knew you called or came by. My mother must have forgotten to tell me. Annie, that means you *do* still love me then?"

"Of course I do. Ned, your mother lied to me. She said you weren't there. She purposely didn't tell you that I called or came by. She's trying to break us up."

"Well, I'm glad it didn't work. I love you so much. Will you wait for me while I'm in the Army?"

"Of course I will, but do you really have to go? Can't you get out of it now?" I questioned anxiously.

"It's too late. I was sworn in today. I leave in a week. Annie, let's get married before I go. Then I'll know I'll never lose you."

"We can't, Ned. When we get married, I want a real wedding, not a hurried-up one. I want bridesmaids and a beautiful gown and flowers, and I want everything to be perfect."

"I know. I'd like that, too. I just don't want to lose you again."

"You *didn't* lose me, silly. And you won't. I don't want to lose you either."

We spent as much time together as possible that last week. I had to go to work during the days, but evenings we were inseparable. We tried to act like things were the same as before, but it was difficult. I couldn't stop crying. I dreaded facing the loneliness again.

Two nights before he was to leave, we were sitting in his car talking.

"Annie, before I go away, I want to make love to you. I want for us to be as close to each other as two people can be. Then we will both have that memory to keep with us while we are apart."

I didn't need convincing. "I want that too. But we have to be careful."

"Don't worry. I'll take care of that. And I'll find the perfect place. Tomorrow night. On our last night together."

"Okay."

Getting through the next day at work was a challenge. I bounced from the heights of anticipation to the depths of depression, knowing the contradictory implications of what that evening held in store for me. I was going to have "real" sex for the first time, but would it all be overshadowed by the thought that it could possibly be my *last* time–my *only* time–with Ned?

# CHAPTER 5

# "Starry, Starry Night"[5]

When Ned picked me up at eight, he seemed so happy, obviously dealing with his upcoming departure better than I. "Let's just enjoy this time together and not think about tomorrow, okay?" I said I'd try.

Elvis was crooning "It's Now or Never" on the car radio as we drove off. *That's appropriate,* I thought. Ned wouldn't tell me where we were going. I quickly realized that my presumption of him getting us a motel room in town was incorrect. We started heading out of town. *Maybe a room in the next town,* I thought. But he soon turned off on a side road, and then another. We were really out in the country. He stopped the car.

"What are you doing?" I inquired.

"This is it. This is where I'm going to make love to you."

"Where are we?" I could see nothing. A blanket of darkness surrounded us. Ned got out of the car and came around and opened my door.

"Come on, I want you to see this," he said, helping me out.

"See what?" I asked, stepping onto the roadside and squinting my eyes in an attempt to see something, anything.

"Close your eyes for a minute." So I did. "Now open them and look up."

---

5. "Starry, Starry Night"; artist: Don MacLean; released 1970.

What I saw was one of the most beautiful and thrilling sights I'd ever experienced. Millions of stars, like cosmic jewels, decorated the night sky. "Oh, Ned, it's beautiful!" He put his arm around me, pulling me close, and we continued staring up for several minutes.

"But here? Are we going to do it here by the side of the road?" I questioned, breaking the silence and bringing us back to the situation at hand.

"No. Come with me and you'll see." He reached in the back seat and grabbed a blanket and a flashlight. "Follow me. And be careful."

I could see that this was going to be a real adventure. First, there was a fence to surmount, topped with barbed wire! Hesitating only briefly, Ned picked me up and lifted me over it. He followed, barely catching his shoe on the descent. Then he took my hand and we began stepping carefully through the tall grasses, led by the beam from his flashlight.

"What if there's a snake?" I suggested.

"Snakes are more afraid of us than we are of them."

I had never believed that old saying, but at that moment it appeased me.

Our path took us up a gentle incline. When we reached the top, Ned stopped and spread the blanket on a grassy patch. "Care to join me?" he asked, flopping onto the blanket.

I lay down next to him, gazing up towards the heavens. Again, I was overtaken by the sight. We lay there quietly for a minute or two, and then he began kissing me. The familiar feelings quickly returned, my body responding immediately to his touch.

I tried to experience every second to the fullest, which made it seem like time was passing in slow motion and yet at warp speed. I wanted to imprint each sensation on my brain so that at any time, I'd be able to call up the memory and relive the entire evening, minute by minute, in my mind.

He went from kissing my mouth to kissing every other inch on my face—my eyelids, my cheeks, and then my entire face, encircling it with kisses, being even more gentle than usual. My neck was next. He slowly worked his way down to my chest, unbuttoning my blouse as he went. My body was coming alive with desire. He reached behind me and unclasped my bra, then paused for a moment, looking into my eyes. My vision had adjusted to the darkness, or maybe the sky had gotten lighter. I could clearly see his face.

"You are beautiful, Annie."

I had never thought of myself as very pretty, much less beautiful. With mousy brown hair and plain features, I was certainly nothing special. When Ned had first called me beautiful—it was just our second date—I was tempted to sarcastically ask him what he wanted from me. But I quickly learned to absorb the compliment and enjoy it. I think Ned really did see me as beautiful, and in fact, I *felt* beautiful when I was with him. This time I could see the love in his eyes as he said it, and I knew he meant it.

Then his mouth was on my breast, and my excitement began to peak. He reached for my waist and fumbled briefly, trying to get my shorts off. I helped him remove them. He pulled my panties down, and his hand was soon swimming in my wetness. He knew my body so well, knew just how to touch me. The next minute, I was bursting with pleasure and moaning wildly.

"Oh, Annie. Annie. Annie. I love when you do that."

I loved it too. He buried his head in my chest, squeezing me tightly, and continued bringing me to ecstasy with his gentle stroking. Each orgasm took me deeper until the physical sensations were all encompassing.

Exhausted, I took his hand, stopping him so I could catch my breath. He sat up quickly and reached for his shorts, lying on the blanket next to him. I had no idea when he had removed them. He retrieved a small packet from his pocket and tore it open. In an instant, he was on top of me, and I guessed, wearing a condom.

"Annie, baby, you are a goddess. I love you so much." He said it softly, looking into my eyes, our noses almost touching.

"I love you too, Ned."

"I don't want this to hurt you."

I could feel him between my legs. "It feels like an egg," I said without thinking.

"An egg?" he repeated. We both started laughing, breaking the tension that we had somehow allowed to develop.

"I'll go slowly," he assured me, beginning to push a little.

I knew I had plenty of lubrication. I hoped that would help.

"That feels good," he whispered softly.

Suddenly a knife was slicing my insides, or so it felt. I tried to suffer silently through the pain, not wanting to ruin it for him. Biting my lip, I felt tears slipping from my eyes.

"Oh, Annie, I could stay inside you forever. You feel so good."

"Be gentle," was all I could say. I continued to endure the discomfort as I felt his body's waves of passion build until they reached their ultimate release.

"Oh god. I'm coming. I love you, Annie."

He remained on top of me as his body relaxed. My pain was subsiding.

"Annie, you're crying. Did I hurt you?"

"A little."

"I'm so sorry. I never want to hurt you. I wanted this to be special for you like it was for me."

"It *was* special," I assured him. "I'm glad it was good for you."

"I love you."

"I love you too." We lay quietly, holding each other. He rolled onto his back, and I snuggled into his arms.

"I wish it could always be like this, our lives, I mean," he said wistfully.

"Me too."

"Look, there's a shooting star!" he exclaimed. "Make a wish."

"I wish that time would stand still so we could stay like this forever."

"You're not supposed to tell!" Ned scolded. "Now it won't come true. There's another shooting star. Make another wish, and this time don't tell."

I wished that he didn't have to leave to go in the Army. I might as well have told because I knew there was no chance of that happening. We saw another one, and I wished Ned would come back after the Army and we'd get married and have two children, a boy and a girl, and live happily ever after. I had a feeling I was asking for a little too much.

Our drive home was somber. I cried all the way. Ned kept telling me that we'd be together again soon, that he'd get leave to come home after boot camp, in just a couple of months. I cried anyway. My sense of impending doom was overshadowing any visions of a happy future with Ned.

# 2011

## BACK IN THE CABIN

Annie stopped writing and looked down at her sleeping pooch. "Let's take a little break, Tulip," she said, trying to bring her mind, and her soul, back to the cabin, and to the present.

"In fact, let's go outside."

After a few minutes outdoors, Annie felt refreshed and was eager to resume her journey into the past. The two of them were soon settled at their posts again, Annie seated at the kitchen table with pen in hand, and Tulip on the floor at her feet.

# Fall 1962

## CHAPTER 6

## "Be True to Your School"[6]

I spent the two weeks following Ned's departure getting ready for college. What should have been an exciting time for me—preparing to leave home for the first time, picking out all the items to decorate my dorm room, shopping for new clothes to last through the year—wasn't. My mother was excited; I just went through the motions. I had an aching numbness. All I cared about was gone, and I couldn't even talk to him. I did write him letters every day and put them in the mail, but I didn't know when or if they were ever delivered to him. Ned had warned me that for his first six weeks of boot camp, I probably wouldn't hear from him much, if at all, and he was right. I tried to sound cheery in my notes to him, but I knew I was bordering on depression.

Finally, I was off to college. Freshman orientation was a welcome relief. The change of surroundings, alone, helped my state of mind, although in some ways, I felt even more removed from Ned. I was now in a place where we had never been together, and it was almost like he and I had existed in a previous lifetime, or maybe only in my dreams. Of course, as a new freshman, I was kept busy with numerous required meetings, lists to memorize, and a whole new set of friends.

I had chosen to attend Martinsburg Women's College (MWC), an all-girls school, about an hour's drive south of Fort Custis. Being around

---

6. "Be True to Your School"; artist: The Beach Boys; released 1963.

only females was actually a good thing for me at that time; many of my new classmates were also missing their boyfriends, and they were eager to share their stories, which meant that they were then obligated to listen to mine. Additionally, because there were no males in residence, I was spared having to endure the sight of happy couples holding hands and strolling around campus each day.

Everyone has probably contemplated, at one time or another, just what would have been the consequences if a certain significant person had not come into their lives when they did. Two schools of thought address this issue. The first would have us believe that any meeting is simply a quirk of fate, that it is a "by chance" occurrence. If they hadn't met when they did, their window of opportunity would be closed. The second explanation is that the two people were meant to cross paths, and if it hadn't happened when it did, another opportunity would have been presented. Taken a step further, they were brought into each other's lives for a reason. They would have met eventually, one way or another.

I had always been inclined towards the latter theory, and if I'd ever had any doubts about that, getting to know my college roommate certainly erased them. She was definitely brought into my life for a reason. I cannot now imagine what my life would have been like without her.

"Hi, you must be Annie. I'm Julia, and these are my mom and dad," she said to me when I arrived that Sunday afternoon. "I've already put my things in this closet, but if you'd rather have it, I'll be glad to switch to the other one." The first of her many caring attempts to make my life easier.

We didn't call her Julia for long. In true dorm fashion, each person had soon earned her own nickname. In most cases, that name stuck throughout the college years, and, in many cases, throughout life, at least in certain circles. As soon as our hall mates discovered that Julia's middle name was Star, she became known as "Ringo," after Ringo Starr of the Beatles, a new young rock group with whom we were all becoming familiar. I don't remember calling her Julia ever again. To this day, she is still my dear friend Ringo.

I must have spent an inordinate amount of time sharing my tragic love story because it wasn't long before my dorm mates began referring to me as "Romeo." I never could figure out why I wasn't Juliet, but for some reason, they decided Romeo fit me better. At any rate, I didn't mind the name. I actually felt a little closer to Ned every time I heard it.

Each evening I made time to share my day's activities with Ned, or at least I would write him and mail it to his Army address. Since I wasn't hearing back from him, it was almost like writing in a diary. We didn't have phones in our rooms, but a pay phone down the hall was available for our use. I repeatedly sent that number to Ned in hopes that someday he'd be able to call. I was counting the days till the end-of-boot-camp leave that he had promised. It was still over a month away.

On the third day of classes, Ringo and I decided to make our first trek to the library. My English prof had given an assignment requiring research, and Ringo said she'd come along to check out the facility. Stopping by there on our way back from the dining hall, I soon learned that books, especially stacks of them, were one of Ringo's passions. Her enthusiasm was contagious, and I found myself developing a new appreciation for the smell and feel of old bindings. We must have spent two hours in the library, investigating the various sections.

Returning to our room, I could see a note taped to our door. It was from our standard message pad and read,

*To: Annie; Caller: Ned Nash; Message: will call back soon; Call taken by: Beth Reynolds; Time of call: 8:53*

I had missed him by five minutes.

Beth lived in the room next door. She and I were calculus buddies, having both skipped freshman math. This analytical ability of hers seemed contradictory to her personality, not what one would expect from such a friendly, outgoing person. She had been a cheerleader and homecoming queen in her high school, not the typical "brainy" student.

Beth was sitting crossed-legged on her bed, with her hair dryer bonnet on her head and painting her nails, when I barged into her room, demanding to know the details of Ned's call.

"He said, 'Hello, this is Ned Nash. May I please speak to Annie Barstow in room 225?'" she explained.

"Then what? Did he say anything else? Is he okay? Has he gotten my letters?" I could hardly get the questions out fast enough.

"He just said he'd try back soon," Beth said. "That's all. I'm sorry."

I sighed. So close and yet so far. *At least he's thinking about me,* I thought. I spent the rest of that evening and, in fact, most of the night going from elation that he had called to despair that I didn't get to hear his voice. When I did drift off to sleep, I dreamed that Ned was there with me. He was looking at me with that sweet, crooked smile, and I wanted so much for him to touch me. I knew that the sparks would begin as soon as our bodies made contact. I could almost feel it. But every time I tried to touch him, I couldn't. He was just out of reach. Frustrated, I woke up in a sweat.

For the next six days, I hardly left the room. I didn't want to chance missing another call. I'd go to classes, of course, but come straight back. Most days, I'd skip lunch and have Ringo bring me something. Two evenings I even missed dinner, settling for a peanut butter and jelly sandwich. On the seventh evening, one week after Ned's phone message, I went to dinner early. I couldn't keep missing meals, and who knew how long it would be till Ned had any free time, as well as access to a phone, again? The dining hall opened at five o'clock and I was waiting at the door, practically the first in line.

Immediately after eating, I returned to the room, settled down on my bed, and opened my books. At three minutes before seven, I heard the hall phone ring. I held my breath, hoping beyond hope. A frantic knock on my door brought the good news. "Romeo, are you in there? It's an LD!" LD meant long distance and was always a big deal.

I was up like a flash and ran to the phone. "Hello?"

"Oh, Annie, it's so good to hear your voice. I only have three minutes. We'll have to talk fast."

"Ned! I miss you so much! I want to see you."

"You will, Annie. Soon. I get out of here in three weeks. I'll come straight there. We should have several days together. I can't wait to hold you in my arms again."

The next two minutes were a blur. Then the operator was telling us our three minutes were up.

"I love you, Annie."

"I love you—" *Click.* We were cut off.

That night, Ned held me close and kissed me for hours—in my dreams. It was so real I could even feel the tingling. At four in the morning, I was startled awake by a slamming door across the hall. I desperately tried to recapture the dream, but it was gone.

Ned was to be there in about three weeks, possibly on a Wednesday. My assignment in the meantime was clear, coming up with a place where we could go to be alone. This was more difficult than it might sound. My dorm room was definitely out. With the exception of an occasional maintenance man, males were forbidden from going any further than the dorm's "parlor" (lobby), a strictly enforced regulation.

Students were required to "sign-out" whenever leaving the campus. This entailed stating exactly where we were going and when we'd be back, at which time we had to "sign-in." We had to return to our dorms, and sign-in, no later than eleven o'clock. The outside door was then locked. We were allowed to sign-out overnight only on Saturdays, and we were not allowed to stay in a local motel (that meant anything within a ten-mile radius of Martinsburg) unless accompanied by our parents. Because Ned and I would not have the use of a car, our options were definitely limited.

Ringo kept reminding me that if Ned and I were going to have any privacy, it was obvious that I was going to have to break some rules. Because we were on the honor system, breaking a rule was a serious offense. One of the crimes for which students could be expelled was lying, and I was fairly certain that signing out for one location and going to another would be considered lying. I did not want to be thrown out of college.

My dilemma was compounded by the fact that I didn't know exactly when Ned would arrive. If he didn't come till Saturday, I figured we could take a bus to a nearby town, like Stafford, which was just far enough away to put us outside the required ten-mile radius. We could get a motel room there and at least have a whole night together.

The problem would be if he came earlier, especially if he had to leave before Saturday. Of course, I was anxious to see him as soon as possible. Two weeks passed, and I still didn't know how to plan. As it turned out, planning wouldn't have helped. I continued to wait and wonder. Wednesday came, and I hadn't heard from him. Wednesday night at two minutes past ten, I got a call.

"It's not good news, Annie," he began. "Some of the guys in my unit messed up, so we're all being punished. I have to stay through Thursday and do some dirty work. I don't even want to tell you about it. But I'd gladly do it all myself if it meant I'd get to see you sooner."

"But you'll be here on Friday, right?"

"Yes, I'll be there Friday. But I can't stay long. There's worse news." He paused. "I got my orders. I'm going to 'Nam. I leave at six o'clock Saturday morning."

I couldn't speak for crying. My universe was collapsing.

# CHAPTER 7

# "With a Little Help from My Friends"[7]

I spent the next day in bed, not really sleeping but not awake either. They told me later that I appeared to be in a trance-like state, where nothing or no one could touch me. Apparently, this was my survival mechanism, creating an escape to keep me from slashing my wrists. I probably would not have even been aware of the disastrous shape I was in if it hadn't been for Ringo. I knew it was bad because she refused to leave my side all day, cutting her classes to stay with me. Since we were only allowed three absences per class each semester, this was a true sacrifice.

Ringo kept my forehead supplied with wet compresses and brought me sips of chicken broth, which she'd heated on our hot plate. She was talking a lot too, but none of it made much sense at the time. By evening, when I began to understand what was going on, I realized she was planning my meeting with Ned for the next day. She had arranged everything for our upcoming rendezvous, down to the last detail. Bless her.

It turned out that Ringo had a classmate who was a Townie, that is, someone who actually lived at a residence in town. There weren't many Townies at our school because most locals chose to go away, if possible, for college. Tina was a sophomore who had met her husband, Ross, right

---

[7]. "With a Little Help from My Friends"; artist: The Beatles; released 1967.

there in Martinsburg, where he worked for the local newspaper. He had been working on a story about life at MWC and had interviewed Tina for the story when she was a freshman. They started dating that summer and, after a brief courtship, got married before she began her sophomore year. Tina and Ringo were in Spanish class together, and Ringo had been to Tina's house a few times to study.

At some point during my bizarre avoidance episode that day, Ringo had called Tina, and they arranged that Ned and I would go to her house Friday night. We would be able to stay there together until whatever time Ned had to leave on Saturday morning. Since off-campus overnights were only allowed on Saturdays, I would have to leave campus without signing out, and the others would cover for me. We could all have gotten into serious trouble for breaking the rules, but none of that mattered at the time. It was the only way that Ned and I would be able to spend any time together.

By Friday morning, my thoughts of Ned were all-consuming. We had never been apart for that long before, and I began to wonder how much he'd changed. I knew he'd lost weight and lost some hair too. Would he still act the same? Would he still love me? Would the sparks still be there?

I made it to my morning classes and even to the dining hall for lunch. When I got back to the dorm, I found a phone message taped to my door. He'd called just after noon. The message read,

*Ned to arrive by 6:00 p.m. Will come to the dorm.*

My last class ended at five o'clock. I figured that if I showered and got ready before the class, I'd still have time to come back, change clothes, and freshen up before his arrival. World history was never one of my favorite subjects, and concentrating was particularly difficult that day. When the instructor dismissed us, I was the first one to the door, virtually flying out of the building and back to the dorm. I was huffing and puffing as I burst through the lobby, heading towards the stairs.

"Where's the fire?" I heard in a familiar voice behind me. Spinning around, I verified the source of what I'd heard. I dropped my books and rushed into Ned's waiting arms. My body relaxed into his, and we stood there holding each other for several minutes, neither of us speaking. His touch and smell were just as I remembered. I knew immediately, the love was still there. The electricity was still there too. For that moment, everything was okay. I was right where I belonged. If only we could have made the moment last.

Ned spoke first. "I love you, Annie. I've missed you so much." Then he kissed me. And I began to cry.

Finally, we found a nearby couch and sat down. Ned explained that he had until about five o'clock in the morning. He had to be on a bus by six that would take him to his flight. He'd fly to California, where they'd keep him for three or four days before sending him to Vietnam.

I couldn't think about that then. I described Ringo's plan for our evening, and he smiled.

"I need to meet her so I can thank her personally," he said.

"Oh, they all want to meet you. They've heard enough about you. And of course, I'm anxious to prove to them that you really do exist."

The plan included Ringo and several others accompanying us for a burger at the campus snack shop. We'd all walk there together, and then, after dark, Ned and I would walk to a drug store off campus, where we could call for a taxi to take us to Tina's house.

I went up to the room and announced Ned's arrival. Ringo and three others were available to join us. Soon, the six of us were off to the snack shop, laughing and chatting like we were all old friends. For a brief time, Ned and I seemed like normal people, people whose lives were not on the verge of devastation.

# CHAPTER 8

# "Back in My Arms Again"[8]

Neither Ned nor I had much appetite for dinner. It wasn't long before we excused ourselves and executed our escape from campus. At the drug store, we made two phone calls, the first to Tina to make sure she was ready for us, and the second, for a cab. At any other time, I would have felt like a criminal under those circumstances, being off campus "illegally." But at that time, all I felt was a desperate need to be alone with Ned as soon as possible for as long as possible.

Tina and her husband were wonderful. After showing us the guest room and encouraging us to make ourselves at home, they left for a movie.

We had so much to say and do and so little time, only about nine hours left before Ned had to go. We lay on the bed, holding each other and not speaking. Eventually, Ned broke the silence.

"I wish we could have gotten married," he said. "At least that way, if I came home in a body bag, you'd be taken care of."

That was not what I wanted to hear. I knew of two MWC students whose boyfriends had been killed in Vietnam. One of those girls had dropped out of school after that, and the rumor was that she'd attempted suicide and that she was still in therapy and couldn't be left alone.

---

8. "Back in My Arms Again"; artist: The Supremes; released 1965.

"I don't want money. I just want you," was all I could say, holding him even tighter.

"If we'd had enough time, would you have married me now?" he continued.

"Oh yes, I would," I answered without hesitation. Getting a marriage license required a three-day waiting period, so I knew it was a purely hypothetical question.

He began kissing me then, long and slow and gently. My body came alive, reacting to his kisses, and I was able to lose myself in the passion and enjoy the moment. His touch was so tender and so familiar. I couldn't allow myself to even consider the harsh reality that this might be the last time we'd ever be together.

His lips began moving down my body, melting every inch of me along the way. So many nights, lying alone in my bed, this was what I had been dreaming about, and now it was actually happening. *Some dreams do come true,* I thought, making a mental note to remember that as if I'd made some profound realization.

He had reached my thighs, and my ecstasy was building as he gradually moved towards the center of my pleasure. Could that be his tongue? I had never experienced such a sensation before, or such intense desire. I began to whimper with anticipation. Finally, with a single slow, warm, well-placed stroke, I exploded into orgasm. The waves consumed my entire being, continuing on and on. I could hear myself groaning. Or was that him? We were both gyrating furiously, causing the bed frame to knock against the wall.

As the contractions subsided and our bodies relaxed, we began to laugh. I'm not sure why exactly, or what was so funny, but it certainly felt good. It was a much-needed relief after being so serious for so long.

"It's a good thing your friends left us alone," Ned stated amid the laughter. "They would have thought I was killing you."

Reality hit me again, and I became very quiet. Ned sensed my thoughts. Pulling me towards him, he began kissing my neck and whispering in my ear.

"I'll love only you for ever and ever. Always remember that. No matter what happens, this night will be ours to relive in our dreams while we're apart."

If Ned was going to be reliving this night over and over, I wanted to make sure that it was truly worth his memories. I climbed on top of him and gently placed my lips on his. Our bodies seemed to merge into a single entity as we kissed. I kissed his neck, his chest, his nipples, working my way down from his muscular pecs to the firm, flat curve of his torso. His body was reacting to me, and I could feel his hardness trying to burst out. Placing my hand there, I slowly unzipped his pants and reached inside. His penis was hot and ready, inviting me to take it. The next thing I knew, I had put my mouth on it. It felt surprisingly smooth and soft to my lips. I gently began licking the end.

"Don't do that if you don't really want to," Ned muttered between moans.

"I do want to," I replied.

"Then don't talk with your mouth full," he teased. His sense of humor was one of the many things I loved about him.

Ned produced a condom from somewhere, and together, we placed it on his throbbing erection. Then I kneeled over him and lowered myself onto him, carefully guiding him into my body. He pulled me down, and our bodies began moving together in perfect rhythm, slowly at first, then faster and faster. I had never felt so close to anyone as our pleasures continued to build simultaneously. The excitement we felt growing in each other magnified our own sensations. The result was incredible as we both exploded into orgasm at the same instant, experiencing a release that seemed to last for several minutes, after which we both collapsed in total exhaustion.

"How can two people be this close one day and so far apart the next?" I asked. "It's just not fair."

"Don't talk about it," was his response. "Let's just enjoy this moment."

So I lay there quietly in his arms, and we must have dozed off. When I woke up, Ned was kissing my eyelids.

"You are a goddess," he whispered. "I want to remember you just like this."

"What time is it?" I asked.

"It's almost four o'clock."

"Oh no, it can't be that late already." I didn't want to believe it.

"I need to take a shower. Do you want to join me?" Ned inquired.

"Of course," I replied, rubbing my eyes and slowly getting up. We had one hour left, and I wasn't going to let him out of my sight. While he went to get the shower ready, I found a towel and wrapped it around my head to keep my hair dry. Acting cautiously, neither of us had brought any extra clothes with us. Ned had left his duffel bag in a locker at the bus station.

"Come on in, the water's fine," he announced as I stepped into the shower. I wondered how he could be so upbeat at a time like that, but I soon discovered that it was just an act. He took the bar of soap, knelt down, and began washing my legs. Then suddenly, he stood up and grabbed me and held me. That's when I realized he was sobbing.

"I'm so sorry, Annie," he managed between sobs. "I'm sorry for all the hurt I've caused you. I'm sorry I have to leave you. I'm sorry I ever joined the Army. I love you so much. I just hope I have the chance to come back and make it all up to you someday."

"I hope so too," was all I could say.

When we got out of the shower, Ned took a towel and gently patted my body dry from head to toe. Then I got back under the covers and watched as he continued drying off and getting dressed. He sat on the bed to put on his shoes, then turned to me and took my hand. Neither of us knew what else to say. I didn't want to cry any more, but I couldn't help it. Tears were streaming down my face.

"I have to find a phone and call a cab," he said quietly. He kissed my hand and got up and left the room. Not wanting him to remember me that way, I tried to compose myself while he was gone but was unsuccessful.

"We have five minutes," Ned said, returning to the bedroom.

"Just hold me," I sobbed. He came over and wrapped himself around me, squeezing so hard I thought I might break. We sat that way, motionless, and I prayed for time to stand still.

Too soon, we heard the cab.

"Don't go," I pleaded. "Please. Don't go."

"I have to. I love you, Annie." And he was gone.

Pulling the covers over my head, I hugged my knees to my chest and bawled. How could I live with such emptiness?

Sometime later, Tina tiptoed into the room. She said she'd be leaving for the campus in a few minutes and that I needed to get up and go with her. That was the plan. Since I had already missed my Tuesday-Thursday-Saturday classes once that week, I definitely needed to attend. Tina would drop me off at the back entrance to my dorm so that I could go in and get my books and make it to my nine o'clock calculus class.

Reacting like a programmed robot, I put my clothes on, splashed cold water on my face, and left with Tina.

# CHAPTER 9

# "I Will Survive"[9]

That first morning was the most difficult, thanks, in no small part, to my calculus professor, Dr. Tobar. Incredibly, I had gotten to class with three or four minutes to spare. My friend Marilyn, sitting behind me, knew of my situation and asked how I was doing. The inquiry precipitated more tears. So I was sobbing, with my face in my hands, when class began. Dr. Tobar was not a compassionate man, to put it mildly. Widely known as "Tobar the Terrible," he certainly lived up to his name that day. His first words upon entering the classroom were "Miss Barstow, to the board!" shouted in a booming voice.

Tobar was notorious for selecting someone who had been absent the previous class period as the first recipient of his wrath each day. I should have been prepared for that, but I was prepared for nothing. Not only had I missed the previous class, but I had also not checked with anyone concerning the assignment, much less attempted to solve the designated math problems. Needless to say, I was at an absolute loss to answer any of his questions.

"Miss Barstow, which is it, A or B?" he demanded. I figured it was worth a guess.

"A?" I offered meekly.

"Miss Barstow, what are you thinking? How could it be A?"

---

9. "I Will Survive"; artist: Gloria Gaynor; released 1978.

"I don't know," I mumbled.

"Miss Barstow, have you read the chapter?"

"No, sir."

"Miss Williams, please go to the board and show Miss Barstow how to do problem 1," he said as the humiliation continued.

Tobar the Terrible did not realize that it was nothing short of a miracle that I was even there, that my heart and soul were hurting, possibly damaged beyond ever being whole again.

A strange phenomenon occurred shortly after that. Apparently, I began acting normal—no more tears, no more signs of depression, and my outlook actually became cheerful. The weird part is that I don't have any memory of that. I have a clear recollection of calculus class that morning, then nothing. Nothing that day, or the next, or for weeks afterwards. It must have been my way of coping with a reality too unbearable to face. Either that, or Tobar's attack at such a vulnerable time had pushed me over the edge, and I just flipped out. Whatever the reason, I was mercifully spared the pain of dealing with the events in my life at that time.

I do have a few selective memories. I remember a phone call from Ned while he was in California waiting for his overseas departure. That must have been Sunday evening, the day after our painful goodbye. It was a brief call, and he even made me laugh at one point when he described one of the guys he'd met on their crowded flight. Corey was a country boy from Arkansas who had never been outside his state before. While the other guys were dreading their imminent tour in Vietnam, Corey kept them amused with talk of his upcoming "Southeast Asia vacation." I remember being glad that Ned had met someone like Corey.

I also have recollections of getting letters from Ned, taking them back to my dorm, and reading them over and over. Those must have been the highlights of my existence. They all had a similar message, that he missed me, that he thought about me all the time, that he couldn't tell me where he was exactly or what was going on there, but that it was "pretty safe" where he was. They came about once every two weeks, sometimes several at a time. They all ended with "I'll love you forever."

Although MWC students were all painfully aware of the Vietnam War, none of us were concerned with the politics of it. It would be several years before students on other campuses began holding the first demonstrations in opposition to the war. Those initial protestors faced arrest and possible jail time for publicly expressing their views, yet their brave actions formed the basis for a movement that spread nationwide, eventually resulting in an end to the war.

We at Martinsburg were not as enlightened or as radical. Even though so many of us were personally affected by the far-away war that we didn't understand, through some sort of strange "mind twist," we never actually "opposed" the war. It never occurred to us to publicly voice opposition to our government's actions. We were not yet ready to challenge the establishment or to push for the change, which would eventually come. Student activism had yet to be discovered.

I never knew how they accomplished it, but the college maintained a board listing the latest Vietnam casualties. Because a large portion of students were involved with soldiers, sailors, or Marines, this was a much-appreciated service (although not one that was promoted to potential students or mentioned in the college handbook). Every afternoon I'd make a trip to the student center to check out the board. I had my own little ritual that I'd perform at each visit, beginning as I entered the building. I'd pretend to be headed to the bookstore, then quickly turn to see the board, almost as an afterthought, exhibiting no more than a casual interest in the names. In truth, I never really expected to see Ned's name listed, but I was just superstitious enough to believe that my daily ritual might be what protected him. At any rate, it seemed to be working. That is, until one afternoon on the way back from lunch.

"How is Ned doing?" my friend Nancy asked as we walked together along the tree-lined pathway between the dining hall and our dorm. "I mean your 'Soldier Boy,'" she added with a grin, referencing a popular song by the Shirelles that I listened to frequently.

"Okay, I guess. I got three letters from him last Tuesday, but they were written several weeks ago."

"Is he in any danger right now?" I wondered why she was asking that.

"I don't really know. He claims he isn't, but that might just be for my benefit."

She was quiet for a minute, then continued carefully. "I'm sure it's not him, but Susana told me she saw a 'Nash' listed on the board this morning."

Fighting off the feelings of dizziness and nausea that appeared from nowhere, I quickly turned and made a dash towards the student center. I must have muttered something to Nancy, but I don't know what.

"I'll come with you," she said, trying to keep up with me.

No ritual this time. I went straight to the board. Walter N. Nash had been added. It *wasn't* Ned. But the realization that *it could have been* hit me like a thunderbolt. I collapsed on the floor, sobbing.

Nancy couldn't understand my reaction. "It's okay. It's okay," she kept repeating. Being happily engaged to a student at nearby Randolph Macon men's college, she was oblivious to the feelings of constant fear that dwelled just below the surface in all of us who had loved ones so far away in that unknown and dangerous land called Vietnam.

The more I thought about it, the worse it became. I was struck with the sudden realization that because Ned's mother had no fondness for me, I would literally be the last to know if something were to happen to him. Unlike others, who would probably receive a phone call informing them of the dreaded news, I would most likely learn it from the board, should that event occur. The board took on a whole new level of significance for me that day.

That sobering afternoon was one of the few detailed memories I have of life that semester. In fact, it was no doubt a major factor in my having very little recollection of college life the remainder of that first year.

# 1963

# CHAPTER 10

## "P.S. I Love You"[10]

Before leaving, Ned had told me many times that I should go out with other people. "There's no reason for you to sit home all the time," he explained. "The college will have lots of activities, and I don't want you to be left out."

I hadn't disputed his statements at the time. I just knew nothing would be much fun if Ned weren't there with me. I didn't want to go out with anyone else. We hadn't discussed it much further than that. So I was somewhat surprised to receive a letter from him towards the end of second semester that was quite insistent on this point, one of my few clear memories from that spring. The following was so unlike Ned's other letters that I found it quite confusing. I never did find out what motivated him to say these things

> *My Dearest Annie,*
>
> *You've never really said in your letters whether you are dating other guys. But I have a feeling from your tone that you aren't. I appreciate more than I can say that you want to be faithful to me, but it seems that I am keeping you from having a normal life at college. I want you to go*

---

10. "P.S. I Love You"; artist: The Beatles; released 1962.

*out and have a good time. It makes me sad to think of you sitting home being unhappy because of me. So will you please stop doing that, for me? Okay?*

*I could be over here for another year, or even more if the war gets worse. That is too long a period for you to isolate yourself.*

*Please write and tell me that you ARE going out with your friends to movies and parties. And don't be sad! Be happy knowing that I love you and that I <u>will</u> come back to you some day and we will be together forever.*

*I love you,*<br>*Your Ned*

*P.S. This doesn't mean I want you to have sex with someone else!*

What on earth did this mean? My first thought was that Ned had found someone whom he wanted to go out with (an Asian woman? an Army nurse?) and he wanted me to be dating too so he wouldn't feel so guilty. But there were seemingly contradictory messages in there. He wanted me to date others and have a good time, but he was worried about me having sex with someone else. I couldn't have imagined having sex with anyone else! Did he want to have sex with another woman? The thought of that made me sick.

I read the letter over and over, studying each word for deeper meaning. Why did he think I was "isolated" and not having a "normal" college life? Many girls at my school were going with servicemen who were deployed; my situation wasn't that much different from the "norm." What had motivated him to write these things?

Of course, I immediately wrote to Ned with all my questions, even knowing that it would be weeks before he would get my letter and respond. By the time he did respond, his only explanation was that he didn't want to be worried about me. What did that mean?

# CHAPTER 11

## "Only the Lonely"[11]

School was over at the end of May, and I returned home for the summer. One of my parents' neighbors worked for the State Department in Washington, and he had assisted me in getting a job there as a summer intern. I started the first of June. A high school friend, Kathy, was also working there. The job itself was somewhat boring, and the long, slow bus ride into the city on a hot, crowded bus was hateful, but working with Kathy made it bearable.

Kathy and I had not been close in high school. We'd had several of the same classes and had studied together a few times. I found her friendly and funny. Her reply to any inquiries about how she landed her summer job with the government was always the same, "Oh, I got the job by sleeping with the president." I guess she was also ahead of her time.

Even though our workspaces were situated in the same area, the office environment did not allow for much conversation during work hours. Lunchtime, however, was a different story. We had an hour for lunch, so Kathy and I began spending that time together. Normally, we both brought sandwiches and we'd go outside to eat them in nearby Lafayette Park. Even on hot days, the chance to get out of the building and get some fresh air was one we couldn't resist. Most importantly,

---
11. "Only the Lonely"; artist: Roy Orbison; released 1960.

these lunch breaks provided me with the opportunity to unload my Ned story on a whole new audience.

Hearing it all for the first time and looking at it as a somewhat unbiased outsider, Kathy was able to offer a different perspective than that of my college friends who had essentially lived the story with me. This could be a good thing. But was it? Kathy was also very blunt.

"You need to get out more, Annie," she commented initially.

"What do you mean?"

"You have very little experience with guys," she explained. "It sounds like you've never really dated, so you have nothing to compare Ned with. Maybe he's only special because he's your first, your only. Here you are, sitting home, pining over this person who's on the other side of the world, when there might be something better right here in your own backyard!"

Did she have a point? "But I don't *want* to go out with anyone else," I protested. "I just want Ned."

"Not only that," she continued as if she didn't hear me. "He *told* you to go out with other guys. Maybe he realizes you all made a commitment too soon. Maybe he wants to see other people and he doesn't know how to tell you."

This thought had crossed my mind once or twice, but I never let it linger. I didn't want it to be true. And none of my dorm friends had ever suggested it, but maybe they just didn't want to hurt me.

"If only Ned were here and I could talk to him in person," I thought out loud, "then I'd know if that were true." *Of course, if he were here, the problem wouldn't exist,* I thought, this time to myself.

"Why don't you let me fix you up with someone?" Kathy said, continuing to ignore my comments. "I know several guys who are just fun to be with."

"I don't know." I tried to imagine it. "I don't really want to, but I guess it would make my mother happy."

"Why do you say that?" Kathy asked.

"Oh, at first, she was fine with me waiting for Ned. She seemed to understand and was supportive. But lately, she's been acting different. And she did this weird thing while I was home over spring break."

"What do you mean?" Kathy was finally listening to me.

"She just happened to have a certain friend of hers, Mrs. Brewer, over for dinner one evening. She is married to a shrink, and he kept asking me questions during dinner, things like how I felt about Ned being so far away, how I felt about his decision to join the Army, and how it makes me feel when I hear about the casualties over there. I resisted his questions initially, but he was so easy to talk to. I guess I ended up spilling my guts to him. I was even crying."

"And what did he do then?" Kathy probed.

"Well, he was nice enough. He kept saying how hard it must be for me. I didn't think too much about it at the time. But later, I heard my mom on the phone with another friend. She was saying that her friend's husband, Dr. Brewer, thought that I was bordering on depression, and that if I didn't get help, I might have a breakdown. She said that she was really worried about me and that she thought the answer was for me to forget about Ned and start seeing other people. She's been nagging me to 'go out and have a good time' ever since, that maybe I would meet another 'nice boy.'"

"So make her happy and do it! I have a friend named Bob. He's a decent guy, and we just hang out. He's kind of like a brother to me. I'll tell him about your situation and that you just want to have a good time. I think you'd really have fun with him. You all could double with Jack and me. We could go to a movie or something. How about Friday night?"

"I don't know. Let me think about it." I knew Kathy had lots of friends, male and female. She and Jack were both well liked. They'd been dating awhile but weren't serious. In fact, she even went out with other guys sometimes. Going out with them seemed like a harmless way to appease everyone. And maybe she was right, maybe it would take my mind off Ned for a little while. But I still didn't want to.

"I'll let you know tomorrow."

I'm not sure if I did it for my mom's sake or just to get her off my back, but the next day, I told Kathy I'd go out with her, Jack, and Bob on Friday. She was pleased and spent the rest of the week talking about what movie we'd see. We finally decided on *The Pink Panther*. I just wanted to get it over with.

To my surprise, Bob turned out to be a nice guy like Kathy had said. And because the four of us stayed together, I wasn't faced with having to make small talk with Bob. The only awkward moment came as we were leaving the theater, and he reached for my hand. Ringo had once shared her philosophy that hand-holding was little more than a means of transportation, but it didn't feel like that to me. Holding hands with someone other than Ned would have felt like a betrayal to him. Bob seemed to understand and didn't try anything else. He was polite and considerate of my wishes. After the movie, Jack suggested that we drive into DC for a beer.

"We can drink there legally, you know," he said, directing the comment to me.

"I know that's true," I replied, "but I'd really rather not. I should probably get on home." I knew the drinking age was only eighteen in Washington, not twenty-one like it was in the surrounding areas. I had heard about the cheap bars that some of my friends had been to, but I wasn't ready to visit one.

"Maybe we can do that another time," Bob said, coming to my rescue. "I'm kind of tired too. Let's call it a night."

Thinking that Bob was probably just anxious to dump his boring, prudish date, I was surprised when he continued.

"We were all talking about driving to the beach tomorrow, Annie. Would you like to go with us? We'll take sandwiches and drinks and make a day of it. The weather's supposed to be great, and if you don't already have plans, I promise you a fun time. I won't try to hold your hand or make you drink any beer, unless, of course, you want to," he said with a smile.

"Oh yes, Annie. It'll be fun," Kathy agreed. "Do it for your mother."

"Your mother?" Bob questioned. "*She's* not invited!" he exclaimed, causing even me to chuckle.

"We'll come by about eight o'clock in the morning," Jack announced when he pulled up to my house. They didn't give me a chance to say no.

# CHAPTER 12

## "Heat Wave"[12]

I didn't want to admit it, but I was almost looking forward to spending a day at the beach with Kathy, Jack, and Bob. It would *have* to be better than another long, lonely Saturday with nothing to do. And my mother was thrilled.

"It's good to see you making plans again," she observed as I was getting out the mayonnaise and looking to see what kind of sandwich materials we had.

"It's just something to do," I defended. But I was ready and waiting a good fifteen minutes before they arrived.

Our drive to the shore was enjoyable, and the time passed quickly. We played those silly traveling games that we all remembered from family vacations in our younger years, counting cars, license plates, and even cows. We laughed, and it felt good.

We found a secluded spot of beach and began unloading the car. I noticed there were two coolers, but I didn't think much about it as we carried our gear onto the beach. The shock came when Jack reached into one of the coolers and I could see that it was filled to the top with cans of beer. There must have been two dozen of them. It wasn't even noon yet. What were they planning? My heart dropped.

"Wow," I said, trying not to overreact. "Are we hosting a party?"

---

12. "Heat Wave"; artist: Martha and the Vandellas; released 1963.

"Just to help us keep cool," Bob explained. "Don't worry. I told you last night that no one would force any on you. But feel free to partake if the spirit moves you," he yelled while racing Jack to the water and leaving Kathy and me alone on the beach.

"This may not have been such a good idea," I said to her. "That's an awful lot of beer for the two of them for one day." I tried to express my feelings without sounding like a total party pooper. "Or is some of it for you?" I continued, in an effort to find out how she felt about it.

"I might have one or two," she replied. "And you might want some too. It will taste really good as the day gets hotter."

That meant she was in on it. I had been ambushed. And what could I do about it? Aside from finding a pay phone and calling my mother to come pick me up, I had few options. I was stuck at the beach with three potential drunks, and I'd just have to make the best of it.

As soon as the guys returned from the water, I suggested that we have lunch, thinking that food would help delay the alcohol absorption in their bodies. Of course, they each grabbed a beer along with their sandwich.

"I'll just have a cola," I said to Bob as he opened the cooler.

"Did anyone bring colas?" he inquired, looking around. Obviously, no one did. All eyes were on me. I knew it was decision time. I quickly ran through my options again. The mother-calling one was definitely out. What choices were left? I could make a scene and demand that we go find me a cola. Or I could be a good sport. They were all waiting.

"I guess I'll have a beer then." *If I couldn't beat 'em, I might as well join 'em,* I thought while silently vowing not to re-enact last summer's beer-drinking fiasco. Since it was the only beverage available, I knew I'd have to be careful. Using the beer to quench my thirst could become a problem. Oh, for a tall glass of water!

I nursed my beer along, taking only little sips, for nearly an hour. By then, it was warm and tasted terrible, so I poured it out. That's when I came up with this great idea. I could keep opening new cans, let them get warm, and pour them out. I should be able to get rid of half a dozen that way, I figured. After disposing of only two half-finished beers, however, I was busted. Bob noticed and suggested that I store my open can in the cooler. That way, it wouldn't spoil and I wouldn't be wasting the beer, he explained. So much for that great idea.

By mid-afternoon, I was feeling the effects. The combination of too much sun, too little fluid intake, and whatever alcohol I'd consumed was giving me a headache. I lay down on the blanket and fell asleep. The nap didn't help. When I woke up, my head was pounding.

Somehow I convinced the others that we needed to leave. They were still enjoying the surf and the beer but agreed to start packing up. I must have looked as bad as I felt. We drove straight to a gas station a few miles down the road, where I purchased some aspirin, which I swallowed along with a gallon or more of lukewarm water from a rusty-looking water fountain. I climbed into the back seat, rested my head against the window, and immediately went to sleep.

I awoke with a start. Something wasn't right. There was a hand on my breast! Bob's body was leaning against mine with his head resting on my right shoulder and his left arm draped around my neck. He appeared to be asleep, or passed out. His left hand was on my breast.

Then I did a strange thing. (I later blamed it on the alcohol. There must have been *some* left in my system, I reasoned.) I didn't move his hand. I not only didn't move it, but I also reached my right hand up onto his, pressing it even tighter against my breast. I closed my eyes and tried to pretend that it was Ned who was holding and caressing me. I wanted so badly to feel that wonderful sensation again, that elusive tingling that sometimes still came to me briefly in my dreams, but to no avail. Nothing. It might as well have been a big, fat, hairy walrus leaning against me.

Thankfully, my parents were out when I got home. I didn't want to explain anything about my "day at the beach," and I knew my mother would ask. I went right to my room, flopped onto the bed, and cried. How different the day would have been if that had been Ned with me. We would have laughed, and hugged, and kissed. Maybe we would have found a secluded spot in the dunes and done more. We would have made plans and talked about our future. Whatever happened to the "carefree days of summer" that I should be enjoying? I asked myself. Where did I go wrong? It was obvious that I never should have agreed to go out with Bob. It only made things worse for me, and it wasn't fair to him either. I vowed not to attempt any more dates. I'd just have to endure my life alone until Ned's return. The immediate future looked so dismal I didn't know how I was going to survive it. If only I could go to sleep and not wake up until Ned was back with me again.

I never did give my mother any details about the beach episode, certainly not because she didn't ask. Her numerous attempts to receive an accounting of my "little beach outing" went unrewarded. I simply told her it was a mistake going out with Bob.

Even Kathy realized it had not been a wise decision. She apologized for encouraging me to go. "I won't pressure you anymore," she promised on Monday.

# CHAPTER 13

## "Nothing but Heartaches"[13]

I did my best to carry out my wish to sleep away the remainder of summer. I did go to work, but aside from that, I slept whenever possible. I went to bed early every night, often without eating dinner. On weekends, I'd sleep late and usually take an afternoon nap as well. I knew my mother was worried about me, but there wasn't much I could do about it. I was trying to make time pass, sleeping and going through the motions of life.

The only exceptions were the two weekends I spent with Ringo. She lived about one hundred miles to the south, near Richmond. She called unexpectedly one evening and said she'd like to come visit for the weekend.

"A toy store near Seven Corners has a doll that my little cousin Jennifer has been asking for. If I drive up on Friday night, we could check out the store on Saturday and then hang out till Sunday, maybe go to a movie or something Saturday night. Jenny's birthday is coming up soon, and I'd really like to surprise her with the doll."

"Sounds great to me," I replied. "I have no plans, and I'd love to see you."

Ringo's visit was the best thing that happened all summer. She arrived about ten o'clock on Friday night, and we talked till after two

---

13. "Nothing but Heartaches"; artist: The Supremes; released 1965.

in the morning. I didn't realize how much I'd missed her. With her, I could be me. I didn't have to pretend about anything. Best of all, she understood about Ned, and she listened patiently while I talked on and on about him, just as if I had seen him yesterday.

She told me about her new boyfriend, Danny, whom she met while working as a camp counselor. He was a counselor also, and they'd had the chance to spend a few evenings together around the campfire.

"He's so outdoorsy and down-to-earth. He wants to be a forest ranger after he graduates, but that may be a ways off. He's having to work his way through school, so it's taking longer. In the meantime, we're just having fun. He makes me laugh, and we do neat stuff like hiking and canoeing, things that don't cost much."

I was happy for Ringo, that she'd found someone so much like herself. At the same time, I couldn't help being envious. I'd give anything to be able to spend a leisurely afternoon canoeing with Ned. *Will I ever have that chance?* I wondered.

The weekend passed too quickly, for a change. On Saturday afternoon, we drove around, and I showed her various places of significance. We even ventured out in the country, and I tried to locate the pasture where Ned had taken me the first time we made love. We drove around and around, but I never was sure I'd found the exact spot; it all looked so different in the light of day. But it afforded me the opportunity to reminisce and relive that memorable night. Ringo was such a dear for enduring my stories and indulging me that way. When she left on Sunday, she made me promise to visit her the following weekend.

"I can't wait for you to meet Danny," she said before backing out of the driveway and heading south towards Richmond.

My weekend at Ringo's wasn't quite as enjoyable. We spent much of it with Danny, and although he was as wonderful as she'd claimed, being with the two of them was difficult. They took me hiking on one of their favorite trails.

"Maybe sometime we can bring Ned and all come back here," Ringo suggested in her attempt to let me know she understood what I was feeling. It was little compensation. I had almost gotten to the point of believing that I'd never see Ned again and that any talk of him was pure fantasy.

We were due to return to college in just two weeks. Both Ringo and I were on the orientation committee and had to arrive early to welcome incoming freshmen. I couldn't get back soon enough. The "all girls" atmosphere provided a safe haven for me. Since no one had their boyfriends there, I could feel like I was almost normal, at least during the week.

I wrote Ned about my visits with Ringo and shared with him how much they made me miss him. I was continuing to get letters from him every week, sometimes two at a time. Those letters served to validate my sanity, proving that he must be a real person after all.

Back in the Cabin

Annie was harshly brought back to the moment when her phone began to ring. Reaching for it, she noticed her younger daughter's name on the screen. "Hi, Ashley!" she exclaimed into the phone.

"Uh, hi, Grannie Annie," replied a youthful voice.

Surprised by the sweet sound of her nine-year-old grandson, Annie responded happily, "Oh hi, Joey! How *are* you?"

"I'm good. I was just calling to see when you'd be back home. Mom and I want to come visit."

"I plan to be home in about ten days, and I'd love to see you and your mom. You can come for the weekend. Your dad too, if he's available. I'll text your mom, and we'll set the date, okay?"

"Okay, Grannie. See you then."

"Thanks for calling, Joey. I can't wait to see you. I love you."

"Love you too, Grannie. Bye."

"Bye, Sweetheart."

Both of Annie's daughters had been especially attentive these last two years, never letting more than a couple of weeks go by without a visit from one or the other. Annie particularly enjoyed the opportunities to spend time with her three grandchildren, and she was most appreciative of her daughters' efforts. She was thankful that they lived so close by, all within an hour's drive.

"Okay, back to the task at hand," she said, pouring herself another cup of tea and returning to her seat at the table.

# Fall 1963

## CHAPTER 14

## "School Days"[14]

It was great to be at college again. I was rooming with Beth, my fellow math major. Since we had shared so many classes and had often studied together freshman year, we'd decided that, for convenience, we'd room together sophomore year. The arrangement worked out well for Ringo too. Her new roommate, Laney, was a fellow English major. The two of them had the room next to ours, with an adjoining bathroom in between, making us all suitemates. Our thought was that Ringo and Laney could stay up late working on their numerous reading assignments and paper-writing without disturbing Beth and me. Math majors had it much easier, we all decided, as long as you could do the math, that is.

Another advantage of living with Beth was that she was practically engaged to a Navy guy who was deployed to the Western Pacific. This meant that she too was pining for a lover who was off to war, although he was probably not in as much immediate danger as Ned since he was on a ship. She hadn't seen Roger for nearly six months, so we had much in common and many similar stories to share. This also meant that neither of us ever had big weekend plans, allowing us to spend weekends together, often just sitting on our beds, composing letters to our far-away boyfriends, hers neatly scripted on her signature butterfly stationery, while mine, although just as heartfelt, were usually penned

---

14. "School Days"; artist: Chuck Barry; released 1957.

on a random piece of notebook paper. We quickly became very close, a match made in heaven as far as roommates go.

However, what started off as a bearable, if not promising, semester soon took a drastic turn for the worse. Barely two weeks after classes started, I received a troubling letter from Ned.

*My Dearest Annie,*

*I don't have much time to write. I'm afraid it's not good news. We're moving out soon to an unknown location, and there's no way of knowing when I'll be able to write again. So please don't worry if you don't hear from me for a while. I'll send you letters whenever possible.*

*Just pray for me—and for <u>us</u>—and let's hope this will all be over soon. Know that you are in my every thought. I live for the day when I'll be back in your arms.*

*I'll love you forever,*
*Your Ned*

I immediately ran back to the room. Beth found me there on my bed sobbing. The letter was wadded up next to me. I had read it so many times I had it memorized. I nodded to Beth, and she picked it up and read it.

"Maybe it doesn't mean anything," she suggested. "There've been other times he couldn't send mail, haven't there?"

"Oh, Beth, how much more can I take? I try so hard to see the bright side, the big picture, as they say. I tell myself there's a reason why we're having to go through this, that it will test our love, or something." I stopped and sobbed some more. Then gaining some composure, I rambled on.

"I don't mean to feel sorry for myself. I know others are going through this too. But it's so hard. I miss him so much, and I don't want to lose him. I keep thinking back to all the chances I had to make things different, and I didn't. I should have married him right after high school like he wanted. Then none of this would be happening. Why didn't I?" And I sobbed some more.

"You couldn't have known." Beth was trying her best to say something comforting. "No one knows why things happen. Sometimes life just stinks. My dad always tells me that challenges make us grow, that we become stronger because of them. So maybe you'll be a really strong person someday . . ." Now she was trying a little humor.

"I don't want to be a strong person. I just want Ned," I blubbered, looking up at her. She couldn't reply to that. I knew that she understood. She had tears in her eyes too.

Ringo and I had coined a phrase one time during freshman year when we were staying up late talking and laughing, doing anything but studying. We'd been discussing the hard life her mother had experienced, how her mother's father had left suddenly when she was just a teenager. Ringo's grandmother had survived and moved on, continuing to raise her children on her own. Her life had been separated into two distinct segments, defined by that one event that had forever changed her grandma's life. When Ringo and I were discussing that situation, we started referring to the time prior to his leaving as "before the bomb." Most of the good memories her mother had of her childhood, for example, had taken place before her father left or before the bomb.

As roommates tend to do (especially at an all-girls school, where excitement is sometimes hard to come by), we had used that phrase to extreme. For example, when the condition of our room had deteriorated to such a cluttered state that we could only laugh about it, one of us would comment, "Remember what life was like before the bomb, when everything was in its place?" And then we'd both go into hysterical giggles in our efforts to escape from the reality of the situation. Those moments of hilarity, along with our massive consumption of rocky road ice cream during desperate times, were major factors in preserving our sanity.

Our "before the bomb" phrase had been used to describe a variety of different situations, some more appropriately than others. My life with Ned, up to this point, had provided too many "bombs," and I wasn't sure if I could handle another. This letter was the latest. After reading it over and over again, I could barely remember what life was like "before the bomb," back when I wasn't completely overwhelmed with worry about Ned's safety. I couldn't even think about what future "bombs" might be in store for him, especially in the immediate future. Possibly *real* bombs.

My self-pity was raging out of control. It seemed that every time I thought things couldn't get any worse, they did. Well, I wouldn't make that mistake again. I knew now that things *could* get worse, the unspeakable could happen. Ned had never asked me to pray for him before, so that had to be his way of letting me know they'd be venturing into enemy territory. Somehow I'd have to force myself not to think about it. Good luck.

Beth had planned to go home the following weekend to attend a family function, but I could see that she was hesitant about leaving me alone.

"Why don't you come with me this weekend, Annie?" she suggested on Wednesday. (Beth was one of the few classmates who actually called me by my real name) "We're having a birthday party for my cousin Frank on Saturday. He's bringing his girlfriend, Janice. You'll like them both. It should be a fun time."

I knew that Beth and her cousin had grown up together, living on the same street. Frank was a couple of years older and was a senior at a men's college in Blacksburg, a town in Southwestern Virginia.

"I won't be very good company," I protested. I didn't want to go and be forced to socialize with anyone. But I knew I'd be miserable staying in the dorm by myself. Both Ringo and Laney planned to be away as well.

"Besides, how can I party when Ned's in such danger? It just wouldn't be right. I'd feel guilty."

"Ned wouldn't want you to sit home and worry. He'd feel bad if he thought you were doing that because of him. And it's not as if your staying here would protect him from the perils of war."

She didn't have to be so blunt. But I knew she was right. "Okay, I guess I'll go, if you really want me to. Thanks for asking," I added.

I had visited in Beth's Southern Virginia upper-middle-class home only one time previously. It had impressed me as stylishly elegant yet not overbearing. In fact, her home was a model for my dreams of what Ned and I would some day create, the all-American home. Her parents were warm hosts, adding to the comfortable atmosphere. You could tell they cared deeply for each other. They too were models of how I imagined Ned and I would be.

# CHAPTER 15

## "Hit the Road Jack"[15]

Immediately after Saturday morning's classes, Beth and I caught the bus for Petersburg. Taking a cab from the bus station, we arrived at her house in mid-afternoon. Her grandparents were arriving at the same time, so we helped them unload their car. Beth's grandmother had brought several casseroles, one of which was baked beans, which I carried in for her. As I entered the kitchen, a male voice advised, "Careful! Don't spill the beans!"

Startled, I looked up to see a pleasant looking tall brown-haired guy, whom I assumed must be Beth's cousin Frank.

"Any more comments like that one and I might," I replied, smiling. "You must be the birthday boy. Happy Birthday. I'm Beth's roommate, Annie."

"Sorry, Annie, I couldn't help myself. It's nice to meet you."

"You too. And I'm anxious to meet your friend Janice."

"Uh, Janice couldn't make it at the last minute."

"Oh, I'm sorry. Beth was telling me how much fun she is."

"Yeah."

Several other neighbors arrived, and after being introduced to all, I excused myself to go unpack.

---

15. "Hit the Road Jack"; artist: Ray Charles; released 1961.

It didn't take me long to figure out that Beth had apparently alerted her family about my situation and solicited their assistance in cheering me up. They all did their best. Her grandma cornered me at dinner and related, in great detail, *her* war story. Her eldest son, Beth's uncle, had been drafted into WWII when he was only eighteen and had spent nearly six months on the battlefront.

"It was the worst time of my life," she told me, her voice quivering with emotion. "I cried every day." The feelings were obviously as vivid to her as if it had just happened last week.

"Thank goodness he came home safe and sound," she concluded with a sigh. "And I'm sure your young man will too," she added, almost as an after-thought, nearly forgetting the original purpose of her story.

I wondered if sometime, forty or fifty years in the future, I'd be relating a similar story to Ned's and my grandchildren. "Your gramps was a war hero, you know. You should be proud of him," I pictured myself saying. Grandpa Ned would be standing there next to me, with his arm around my waist, and we'd be laughing about the hard times we had lived through "back then."

Even the honored guest made an attempt to console me. After dinner, I was sitting alone on a patio bench, working on a piece of birthday cake, when Frank came over and sat down next to me.

"I can tell your mind is elsewhere," he began. "It must be hard to carry on a long-distance relationship, especially under such adverse conditions."

"Yeah, it is," I said, always glad for an opportunity to talk about my favorite subject. "The last I heard from Ned, it sounded like he'd be involved in some dangerous activities. It's hard not to worry about him. Plus, it makes it difficult to get into a party mood."

"I can imagine," Frank offered. I guess he didn't know what else to say. But I had lots more.

"We haven't seen each other in nearly a year. Sometimes I wonder if I'll ever see him again."

"Of course you will. Shouldn't he be home soon?"

"Well, you'd think so. Normally, he would, but he had to transfer units, for some reason I'll never understand, so he didn't get leave."

"How much longer will it be? Does he have any idea?" I'm sure Frank wasn't truly interested but was just making conversation.

"If he does, he's not sharing it with me, so it's probably not good news. Another six months or even a year, for all I know."

"That's terrible," Frank said.

We sat quietly for a few minutes, then Frank spoke again. "Would you like to dance?"

Caught off guard, I looked to see if he was kidding. As if to prove he wasn't, he stood and took my hand, leading me to the center of the patio, where several others were swaying to the sounds of Elvis that were drifting out through the trees. I never did give him an answer, but I didn't resist either. Dancing with him would be safe, I reasoned, since he was committed to Janice. I guessed that he had reached a similar conclusion about dancing with me.

Elvis was crooning "Are You Lonesome Tonight?" just for us, it seemed. We danced in silence, each of us dreaming of someone else. It did feel good to be held again, though, and Frank was a good dancer. When the record ended, I quickly thanked him and went to find Beth.

Beth was involved in a lively discussion with several of her relatives. Not wanting to interrupt, I went straight to the bedroom. Beth's room was a holdover from her high school days. She had twin beds with pink gingham bedspreads and a dresser and vanity set, both white with gold trim. Her purple and white pom poms were tacked to the wall above her cheerleading photo. It was quite a contrast to my room with its plain brown furniture and brown plaid bedspread. Being in her room felt like living in a storybook, which fit right in with the rest of the house. To me, it was the perfect, magical, fairytale-like home, ranch style with a finished basement that included knotty pine walls, a ping pong table, and a built-in bar for entertaining. There was a lovely screened-in porch on the side of the house and a modern kitchen outfitted with matching yellow stove, refrigerator, and dishwasher. Everything was color coordinated, from the green and purple flowered couch and the green shag carpet in the living room to the yellow touches added in the kitchen's wallpaper. It was like a dream.

This was what I'd write Ned about, I decided, as I slipped on my robe, unpacked my pen and paper, and settled myself on the cozy bed in a nest of pink pillows. I described the house to him in great detail, including a drawing of its layout. I drew furniture in each room, arranging it the way I envisioned Ned and I would want it. The master bedroom I labeled "Ned and Annie's private place." In the other bedrooms, I wrote "Ned Junior" and "Annie Junior" That was sure to make him smile, I thought.

I mentioned the Elvis music and how it made me feel. I didn't include that I was dancing with someone else though. I thought about telling him that dancing with another guy only made me miss him more, but I decided that he might take it the wrong way, and I definitely didn't want that to happen.

Sleep overtook me shortly after that. I slept soundly until almost seven in the morning, when I awoke with terrifying thoughts of Ned. I imagined him on the battlefield, dodging enemy fire and explosions. The vivid images raced through my mind like a movie in fast motion. I tried to replace those images with thoughts of him holding and kissing me but was not successful. I noticed that Beth was still sleeping, so I got up quietly and followed the aroma of freshly-brewed coffee down the hallway to the kitchen, where I found her father absorbed in the Sunday paper.

"Good morning, Mr. Reynolds," I said.

"Oh hi, Annie. Did you sleep well?"

"Very well, thanks. That was a great party last night."

"I'm glad you enjoyed it. Help yourself to some coffee. We'll be having breakfast in about an hour."

"Is there something I can do to help?" I asked.

"I don't think so, Dear. Beth's mother and I have it down to a system. You just relax."

"I'll go shower then," I said, wondering if Ned and I would ever be so established in our lives with each other that we'd have fixing breakfast together "down to a system." I wanted to go back and ask Mr. Reynolds if he had any idea how fortunate he was that he had such a perfect life, a wonderful family, a beautiful home, and this great relationship with his wife. *They are living the American dream,* I thought. *I wonder if they know it.*

Frank had spent the night also, sleeping on a twin bed in Chip's room, Beth's brother. He was just coming out of the bathroom when I went in to shower.

"Good morning, Annie," he said, smiling. "Sleep okay? You must have gone to bed early."

"Hi, Frank," I replied. "Yeah, I guess I was really tired."

"Dancing with me wore you out, huh?" he continued, teasing. "And we were making such beautiful music together."

"What?" I said without thinking. Then I quickly went into the bathroom and shut the door. *Was he flirting with me?* I wondered.

I kept my distance over breakfast, and Frank didn't say anything else suggestive, so I guessed he had just been kidding earlier. And possibly, no, *probably*, I was being super-sensitive.

Beth and I left about noon for the bus station and the ride back to school. It was a somber trip. The thought of returning so early on a Sunday afternoon to a somewhat deserted campus, as well as having to face the class assignments we'd ignored all weekend, combined to create our solemn moods. On top of that, I was concerned about Ned, and Beth was missing Roger. We were pretty quiet.

She finally broke the silence. "It's too bad about Frank and Janice," she said.

"Yeah," I replied. "Why didn't she come with him? Did he say?"

"She broke up with him. Didn't he tell you? He thought things were fine when, out of nowhere, she announced that they were getting too serious and they should start seeing other people. Just last week. He was really upset."

"Wow," I said. "If I'd known that, I'm not sure I would have danced with him."

# CHAPTER 16

## "Please Mr. Postman"[16]

Unfortunately, my dance with Frank was the most excitement I'd have for a while. As hard as I tried to keep negative thoughts of Ned out of my mind, they were always there. And nothing happened to dispel them. No letters. No word from him at all. I couldn't concentrate on my classes, reflected by my falling grades. The feeling of impending disaster wouldn't go away.

I finally resorted to calling Ned's parents. Certainly, they should know if he was all right. Preparing myself to talk to his mother, I was shocked to hear a recorded message stating, "The number you dialed has been disconnected." Not believing it, I dialed again and got the same result. *How can this be?* I thought. Ned never said anything about them moving. *What is going on?*

I was panicked. By the time I got back to my room, I was screaming. "Why is this happening to me?" I yelled. "I can't take any more! Ned's probably dead! I might as well kill myself!" And then I started crying. Beth watched in disbelief.

Coincidentally, my parents called later that evening, and I dumped it all on them. My mom didn't say much, but my dad said he'd see what he could find out about Ned for me.

---

16. "Please Mr. Postman"; artist: The Marvelettes; released 1961.

"I have a couple of friends in important places," he said. "They might be willing to help."

"That would be great, Dad. Thanks," I said. "I'd feel so much better if I just knew he was all right."

Then they said they'd be coming down for a visit on Sunday afternoon and would like to treat Beth and me to dinner.

"Okay," I replied. "I'll invite her. And I hope you'll have some good news for me." For once, I was grateful for their involvement. I knew then that I could make it through the week.

Two days later, when I returned from dinner, I found a phone message from my dad. "Call back when you can," it read. I ran immediately to the pay phone and made the collect call.

"Yes, I'll accept the charges," I heard him tell the operator.

"Dad, did you find out anything?"

"Hi, Annie. Yes, my friend at the Red Cross did a search and found no record of a Ned Nash on any of the missing, injured, or fatality lists. My other friend at the Pentagon talked to a general that he knows, and they seem to think that his unit has seen some action but with very few casualties. They say he's probably fine, just out of contact."

"Oh, Dad, are you sure? I hope that's true."

"We'll see you on Sunday, Dear," my dad concluded, "mid-afternoon."

"Okay. See you then. Thanks, Dad. I love you."

"I love you too, Sweetheart."

I hung up, leaned against the wall, and began sobbing. "Please let it be true," I prayed.

After this conversation, Sunday afternoon's dinner with my parents lost some of its appeal. I had found out what I needed to know. Ned was just out of contact, not dead. However, going out with them would provide an escape from the routine for both Beth and me, and just maybe there'd be some other news.

Mom and Dad arrived at the dorm promptly at three o'clock Sunday afternoon, and we left immediately for the nearby Hot Shoppe.

"I'm hungry as all get out," my dad announced as we settled into a booth. "Let's order first, and then we'll talk." Since Beth and I had slept in and had eaten nothing but peanut butter crackers, we readily agreed. After we'd ordered, my dad told us that he'd done some further investigating.

"I've been trying to locate Ned's parents," he said. "It's very strange. No one seems to know where they are. I talked with several of their old neighbors and learned that they moved about two months ago, possibly to Arizona. Mr. Nash had taken early retirement because of poor health. The move resulted from that and was kind of sudden. Surprisingly, no one had a forwarding address. They must not have been close to any of their neighbors."

He paused for a moment and then continued, lowering his eyes a bit. "Annie, I know you want to keep in touch with them in case there's any news of Ned that you'd want to be informed of. My suggestion is to send a note to them at their former address. Surely, their mail is being forwarded to their new location. Let them know of your concern, and ask them to keep you apprised of any news. Certainly, they would understand and cooperate."

"Okay, that's what I'll do," I agreed, reflecting that my dad didn't know Ned's mom very well.

Our meal together was enjoyable. Beth and I put up with my father's attempts at humor, and we both overate, each of us finishing with a hot fudge sundae.

"This meal has to last us till you come back again," I said for their benefit and which they seemed to appreciate.

"Speaking of meals," my dad jumped in, "your mom and I are thinking about going to visit your Uncle Robert for Thanksgiving. They've been asking us to come. We haven't seen his family for nearly two years. We'd take a week, drive up to New Hampshire, and do a little sightseeing along the way. We know you couldn't be gone that long, and we don't want to leave you with nowhere to spend the holiday. Do you think you could go home with someone?"

"She can come home with me!" Beth exclaimed without a pause. "We'll have a great time. And don't worry, I'll take good care of your little girl."

"Fine with me," I agreed, not mentioning my view of the Reynolds as the ultimate in families. I couldn't think of a better place to spend Thanksgiving.

My mother had been fairly quiet all afternoon up until Beth said her goodbyes and went back to our room, that is. My parents and I were sitting in the dorm's parlor when I was blindsided by her comments.

"Annie, dear," she began. I should have known at that point that I was in for a lecture. "We are so worried about you. You're just not yourself. Your grades have fallen, and you don't laugh like you used to. We think that you're making a big mistake basing your whole life around that young man. He made his choice, and it wasn't to be here with you. He chose to join the Army and go away. You musn't waste your life waiting for him. You ought to be seeing other boys and enjoying your college years. If he thinks you should be spending your days just pining over him, he's got another think coming! I'd like to tell him a thing or two!"

I could see she was getting upset, so I tried to stay calm. "I know how you feel, Mom."

"Please think about not limiting yourself so," she said after a brief pause. "You need to perk up and get back to being your old self. If he really cared about you, he wouldn't want you to be making yourself so miserable."

"I'm okay," I said. "You don't need to worry." I couldn't promise anything to her, and she knew it. She also knew I *wasn't* okay.

That evening, I composed a note to Ned's parents. After scratching out and rewriting a number of times, I was finally satisfied that it was sufficient, not too desperate or demanding but strong enough to get their attention.

> *Dear Mr. and Mrs. Nash,*
>
> *I am hoping that this letter will reach you at your new address. I understand that you have moved to another state for health reasons, and I hope you are both doing well following the move.*

*As you know, Ned and I love each other and are planning a future together. However, because we don't have an "official" relationship, if anything were to happen to him, I would not be notified. Therefore, I am enclosing my address and phone number and am asking you to please let me know in the event that you receive any notifications about him. I sincerely hope and pray that this will never happen.*

*Thank you for your consideration.*

*Sincerely,*
*Annie Barstow*

I read it one more time. *Sounds kind of stiff,* I thought. But I didn't want them to think I was getting too familiar. What I was asking seemed clear enough, and that's all that really mattered. I added a card with my addresses, both at home and at school, as well as both phone numbers, and I placed it in an envelope and sealed it. I mailed it the next day.

The following Friday, I hit the jackpot—five letters from Ned! They had been written over a period of about a month, the latest only a week before. Obviously, the earlier ones had been held somewhere. I read the latest first, tearing into it to make sure nothing had changed between us. "My Annie, I love you so much," I saw at the end. Once I read that, nothing else mattered. He was okay, and he still loved me. I was walking on air for the rest of the day.

# CHAPTER 17

## "In the Midnight Hour"[17]

Saturday evening, Beth and I went into town to see the new Beatles movie, *A Hard Day's Night*. We were in a silly mood after that and decided to walk back to the campus, laughing and giggling all the way. Continuing our revelry when we returned to our room, we brought out the chips and Cokes and began playing cards. We had switched to backgammon and were deep into the game at two o'clock in the morning, when there was a frantic knock on our door. "Romeo, LD!" I thought I was dreaming. Then my senses kicked in, and I was off the bed, out the door, and bolting down the hall.

"Hello? Hello?" No response.

"Hello?" I tried again.

"Annie, are you there?"

"Ned?" I couldn't believe it. "Where are you?"

"I'm in Hong Kong, on leave. We have a week. I slept for the first three days. We only have a few days left now. Of course, I was hoping I could come home, but there's just not time."

"It's so good to hear your voice! I can't believe I'm really talking to you! You sound the same. I love you so much."

"I love you too, Annie. But . . ." And then he hesitated.

"But what?"

---

17. "In the Midnight Hour"; artist: Wilson Pickett; released 1965.

"Oh, Annie, I just think it would be better if you didn't wait for me."

"What do you mean?" I stammered.

"It's not fair to you. I'm ruining your life. I want you to start living like a normal college student, go to parties, go out with guys. Have a good time and stop thinking about me."

I didn't know what to say. Where was this coming from? "Ned, what are you really saying? We don't have a future together?"

"You can't count on that, Annie. We don't know what will happen. Please, for me, do this. Tell me you will."

"Tell you I'll go out with other guys? Is that what you want?"

"Yes, it is."

I was paralyzed. For a moment, all I could feel were the tears rolling down my cheeks and dripping off my chin. I couldn't speak.

"I think it would be best for now," he continued.

This wasn't the Ned I knew. This couldn't be happening.

"I-I don't understand," I said, trying to make some sense of this nightmare. I forced myself to ask the obvious question. "Do-Do you want to go out with other people?"

"I think we both should. It would just make things easier."

"Easier? What things?" I was getting more and more confused.

"For us both. It's too hard this way."

"Can I still write to you?" I questioned.

"Yes, of course, you can. And I will keep writing to you too whenever I have the chance. Just don't make it your whole life, okay?"

"You *are* my whole life." I was crying again.

"Well, I shouldn't be. I'm not there for you, and you need to think about other things."

"I don't want to think about other things," I protested. "I love *you*. Nothing else matters." I knew I was beginning to sound whiney, and I hated that. I tried to get control. Whining was only going to drive him further away.

"Everything else matters," Ned said. "Your classes, your social life, your friends—"

"If you want to break up with me, just say so," I interrupted in an attempt to force him to tell me what was going on.

"It's not that."

"Then what is it?"

"I told you. You need to be getting on with your life and not thinking about me. The best way for you to do that is to go out and have fun with other people."

"And you?" I asked again. "You'll go out with other people too?"

"There's not much 'going out' where I am," he said, "but yes, if I have the opportunity."

I couldn't take much more. I was feeling nauseated. "Please explain this to me in a letter, okay? I still don't understand it."

"Okay, but I don't know how to make it any clearer."

"Well, please try. I love you so much."

"I love you too, Annie. And I'm sorry I've hurt you. Goodbye."

"Goodbye," I muttered. What did he mean by "hurt you"?

So many unanswered questions in my mind and Beth was already asleep when I got back to the room. I resisted the temptation to wake her to help me figure this out. Instead, I lay on top of my bed and went over and over his every word, trying to find the hidden meanings. In the end, I was convinced that Ned had met someone else, had sex with her, and was feeling guilty about it, so he wanted me to do the same. That would explain all his comments. My revelation was so depressing I wished I hadn't figured it out, but by then, I was too numb to even cry anymore. Overcome by exhaustion, I finally fell asleep just as the sun's rays were bringing the first signs of morning.

# CHAPTER 18

## "Tragedy"[18]

All things considered, I found myself handling this latest "bomb" amazingly well. My premonition of doom had been realized (although not in the manner that I had anticipated), so in some weird way, it was almost a relief. I didn't have to hold my breath any more; one of my greatest fears had come to pass. And as much as I still loved Ned, my thoughts of him were beginning to take on a new aspect. Resentments were starting to creep in. He had chosen to leave me and go into the Army, which, in turn, had caused me unbearable heartache. How could he have done that if he truly loved me? And now this. He was telling me not to wait for him. Perhaps he *didn't* really love me. Maybe his mother was actually right—we had gotten too serious too soon.

These were my jumbled musings as we prepared for Thanksgiving break. The prospect of celebrating the holiday with the Reynolds family and enjoying four days of their hospitality provided a glimmer of light in my future.

And then another bomb dropped, this one on the national level. It happened the week before Thanksgiving. Every detail of that bizarre afternoon is as clear to me as if it happened yesterday. Beth and I were returning from lunch. We had gone off campus to a sandwich shop across the highway from the college and had made the leisurely trek

---

18. "Tragedy"; artist: the Bee Gees; released 1979.

back through the campus, enjoying the sunny November afternoon. Entering our dorm, we could hear yelling throughout the halls, our first sign that something was wrong. Then Ringo appeared. She was screaming, "The President's been shot!" I thought she was kidding until we got close enough to see the tears on her face.

"Come, listen!" she demanded, leading us to her room, where a crowd was gathered around the radio. We joined the others, listening with disbelief, to the details of the shooting of President Kennedy.

Life at MWC was, for the most part, a sheltered experience. Other than the Vietnam War, events in the outside world had little effect on our daily lives. On November 22, 1963, that changed. Every person on campus was personally affected by the assassination of John F. Kennedy. Most of us cried, all classes were canceled, and many students attended impromptu church services, not knowing what else to do with the feelings this horrible national crisis had evoked.

Beth, Ringo, Laney, and I walked over to the nearby Episcopal Church, where my math professor, Dr. Roberts, served as the presiding priest. More memorable than his service that day was the stark realization to all of us of how short life is and how quickly everything can change. I think we each grew up a little that afternoon.

Classes were canceled again the next day. Being so close to DC, many students chose to become a part of history, going to Washington to view the funeral procession in person. The four of us, however, decided to remain on campus and mourn together, not just for the loss of our President but for the loss of our innocence as well.

# CHAPTER 19

## "Apples, Peaches, Pumpkin Pie"[19]

The following week, a numbness permeated the student body. Everyone seemed to be going through the motions of college life while still trying to process the week's strange events. In some perverse way, I found that I was almost grateful for the timing of this national tragedy (certainly *not* for the tragedy itself). Not only had it served to distract me from my personal circumstances, but it also gave me comfort to know that all the country was experiencing a loss along with me. Somehow it helped lighten my load.

By noon on Wednesday, the day before Thanksgiving, the campus was nearly deserted. My afternoon geography class had been canceled, so Beth and I were free to leave for Petersburg as soon as we could finish packing. We planned to catch the two-o'clock bus. I was actually excited, which Beth picked up on.

"You're in a cheery mood," she noted as we were throwing things into our suitcases. "Just glad to get out of here, or did you receive some good mail?"

"It must be the former because it's definitely not the latter," I replied. "I haven't gotten anything from Ned since the phone call. He's on leave, and he doesn't have time to write? That tells me something, don't you think?"

---

19. "Apples, Peaches, Pumpkin Pie"; artist: Jay & the Techniques; released 1966.

"Not necessarily." My friends were always so supportive, or at least tactful, when it came to Ned. "Remember when I didn't hear from Roger for nearly a month? I was worried at first, then angry. And it turned out, it wasn't his fault after all. There was that helo that went down with everyone's mail on it. So don't jump to any conclusions."

"I'm not exactly jumping. He told me how he felt on the phone. And it's okay. If he wants it to be that way, I'm glad he told me. I wouldn't want to be sitting around waiting for him if he didn't plan to come back to me."

"Wow! You are handling it well. Maybe it will be for the best in the long run."

"That's hard to hear, but you could be right. At least it's forcing me to move on. This may sound stupid, but I really believe that if we're meant to be together, then it will work out. If not, then the sooner I accept it, the better off I'll be." I could hardly believe what I was hearing myself say. *Do I really feel that way?* I pondered.

"Then maybe it's time for you to go out with someone else," Beth offered. "I could fix you up this weekend. Everyone from high school should be home for Thanksgiving."

"I don't think I'm ready for that yet. But thanks. Now let's call a cab and start our vacation!"

"Welcome, Annie. We're so glad you could join us again," Mrs. Reynolds was greeting us at the door. "Come on in and get settled."

"Thanks for having me," I replied. "It smells like a French bakery in here!"

"It's just some pumpkin pies I'm baking for tomorrow. And a couple loaves of bread."

*This is the way I want my house to smell,* I thought, making a mental note to learn how to bake pies and make bread so that someday I could provide these same welcoming aromas to guests in my home. Funny thing, I noticed that my images of a future home and family still included Ned as part of the vision. I realized that deep down, I was still convinced that Ned and I would eventually be together.

"Is there something we can do to help?" I inquired.

"Not now, thanks," Mrs. Reynolds said. "But tomorrow morning, there'll be lots to do. How are you at peeling potatoes?"

"We're trainable," Beth answered for both of us. "Just call if you need us, Mom," she continued as she directed me down the hall to her room.

Thanksgiving Day was wonderful. Not just the meal, although that was great, but also the warmth of Beth's family. I was the only "outsider," but they all made me feel so welcome that I kept forgetting that I wasn't actually a part of the family. Besides Beth, her parents, and brother, there were her grandparents and her cousin Frank and his parents, (Beth's and Frank's fathers were brothers.) After we were all seated around the table, Beth's father got our attention to make a little speech.

"Before we partake of this fabulous spread, I want to say how grateful I am to have all of us together again, and I especially want to welcome Annie to our table."

"Thank you," I responded. "I can't think of anyplace I'd rather be," I added truthfully.

"And I'd like to make a toast," he continued, raising his glass of cranberry juice. "To happy times with family and friends."

"Hear, hear." Everyone joined in, and the feasting began.

"Everything's just delicious," Beth's grandmother said after a few minutes. "Did you do all this yourself, Dear, or did the children help?" she asked Beth's mother.

"Oh, they all did their part. Chip helped stuff the turkey, Beth was responsible for the green bean casserole, and Annie had a hand in the mashed potatoes."

"Annie's hand was in the mashed potatoes?" Frank spoke up suddenly. Then he added with a grin, "No wonder they taste so sweet." While everyone was chuckling over that, I was having a déjà vu moment. Once more, I wondered if Frank was flirting with me. I searched for a response that would gracefully change the focus of his comment.

"Oh, that must be from the rose-scented hand lotion I used this morning," I said, looking directly at Frank. Everyone laughed, and that topic was over.

Being an only child, I had never experienced a real family Thanksgiving before, and now I knew what I'd been missing. One time a few years back, we did have my Uncle Robert, my mother's older brother, and his wife and sons, but they were more like guests than family. Dinner with the Reynolds clan was a true family experience, and I loved every second of it. The food was tasty and plentiful and the conversation casual and cheery. First subconsciously, and then very consciously, I knew that this was the kind of tradition I hoped Ned and I would establish someday. *Our children should have the security brought about by this kind of family togetherness,* I reflected.

After dinner was over and clean up completed, Beth's brother, Chip, brought out the board games, and somehow I was coerced into a Monopoly match with Beth's mom, Chip, and Frank. Frank's mother, his grandfather, Beth, and her father went for the Scrabble. We played for what seemed like hours until we were all feeling the effects of too much food and too little activity. As the yawning increased and our eyelids got droopier, the day's activities drew to an end.

Before leaving, Frank hesitated at the door for a moment then looked at me and said, "I was thinking of going to Richmond tomorrow evening to see *The Sound of Music*. Would you and Beth like to come along?"

I looked at Beth, and we responded in unison, "Sure."

"Good. I'll find out what time it starts and let you know when I'll be by to pick you up."

At six fifteen Friday evening, Frank arrived, driving his parents' Ford Fairlane convertible with the top down. All three of us sat in the front, me in the middle. The wind and road noise made conversation difficult, so Beth and I sat back and enjoyed the ride. Frank's driving was superb. He was not one to show off or take unnecessary chances. The wind in our hair gave a feeling of freedom. We felt carefree but not foolish or crazy.

We had a few minutes' wait in the theater lobby during which Frank ran into a friend from school.

"Hey, Frank, how did you get TWO such good-looking dates?" we heard from a tall dark-haired guy who was holding hands with an attractive blonde.

"Hi, Doug. Guess I'm just lucky. But they're not actually dates. These are my cousins, Beth and Annie. And this is my friend Doug and his fiancée, Fran," he continued, turning towards us.

"They're both your cousins? What a family you have!" replied Doug.

"Well, sort of," Frank said. "Beth is my cousin, and Annie is her roommate, but they're both practically engaged to military guys. I'm just their escort for the evening."

"Glad to hear you're doing your part to support our troops," Doug quipped. "Have a great evening," he added as he and Fran headed towards the popcorn counter.

We found seats near the center of the theater, and as it worked out, I was again situated between Beth and Frank. I couldn't help but wonder if this was a pre-arranged plan on their parts, but I quickly dismissed that thought. If Frank were interested in being something more than friends, he wouldn't be referring to me as his "cousin," I told myself. Having decided that, I actually felt quite safe nestled between two such good friends, and I totally immersed myself in the movie.

After the show, Frank suggested that we stop at the nearby Big Boy drive-in for a snack. "The place will be crazy with high school kids, but since we don't know them, who cares? Let's put the top down and get into the spirit of things," he said, turning up the volume on the radio.

Neither of them had seemed to mind that I had managed to be the last one in the car, putting Beth in the middle. The three of us sipped chocolate milkshakes and sang along with the blaring music. I couldn't remember when I had felt so relaxed and uninhibited.

"I had a great evening. Thanks so much for taking us," I said to Frank when he dropped us off at Beth's house an hour later.

"It was my pleasure," he replied, smiling. "Maybe we can do it again sometime."

# CHAPTER 20

## "You've Got a Friend"[20]

Beth suggested that we devote Saturday to studying for our upcoming exam in advanced calculus, a class that neither of us was going to pass if we didn't soon catch on. We spent most of the day secluded in her room, going over problems and quizzing each other. Our thought was that even if we couldn't understand the work, we could possibly get by if we just memorized all the homework assignments. We were exhausted when her mother came in about four o'clock and announced that Frank and his parents would be over for an early dinner. Any excuse for a break was fine with us at that point, so we gladly put our books away and then drew straws to see which of us would shower first. I won.

Dinner was like Thanksgiving all over again, only now it was turkey divan, which Beth's mother had made from the leftovers.

"This is really good, Aunt Ruth," Frank said after the first few bites. "Did Annie have her hand in it too?" This time I chuckled, along with everyone else.

After the meal, Beth's mother announced that dessert and coffee would be served in the living room. Beth and I helped her clear the table and start the coffee. In a few minutes, we were all comfortably settled around the fireplace enjoying the parfaits that Mrs. Reynolds

---

20. "You've Got a Friend"; artist: James Taylor; released 1971.

had apparently assembled earlier in the day. All was quiet except for the crackling of the fire and the clanging of spoons against glass.

It was the perfect time for me to thank my hosts. "This has been a wonderful Thanksgiving," I said. "Thank you all so much for letting me share in your family's holiday."

Beth's father was the first to respond. "We've enjoyed having you. And Christmas is next. You're welcome to join us for that too, if you'd like."

"Oh, thank you. I'd love to. But I'm afraid my parents wouldn't understand if I weren't with them for Christmas."

A few minutes later, Frank's parents got up to leave. They had been invited to another party. Beth's mother asked Chip to help her with the dishes, and Beth went with her father into his study to discuss her finances for the rest of the semester. Only Frank and I were left by the fire, the first time we had actually been alone together all weekend. I was sitting on the couch, and he was sitting on the floor in front of the couch. In another moment, it was going to be an awkward situation.

"I thought they'd never leave," Frank said, getting up and moving to the couch. He sat at the other end and turned towards me. "Guess I didn't pay them enough," he continued with a grin.

"And just what are you planning?" I asked, trying to match his lighthearted tone.

He got serious then. "Oh, Annie, I only say those things to cheer you up. I understand that you're committed to someone and waiting for him. Don't you know I'm just kidding?"

"Are you?"

"Yes, I really am. And if it makes you uncomfortable, I won't do it anymore."

"It's okay." I didn't know what else to say.

"You *are* still waiting for him, aren't you?" he asked.

"I . . . well . . . I'm not sure exactly. It's so confusing and so hard to communicate when he's that far away. I'm not sure where we stand right now. I know I still want a future with Ned, but I don't know what he wants."

"Why? What happened?" Frank inquired.

"He called me from Hong Kong. He was there on leave."

Frank jumped in then. "He had leave and he didn't come home?"

"Yes, well, he said he wanted to, but there wasn't enough time. Then he went on to tell me that we should go out with other people and that I shouldn't wait for him any longer. He says he still loves me and that he's sorry for hurting me. I just don't get it."

"That *is* confusing. What do you think it means?"

"I'm not sure. I asked if he was saying those things because he wanted to go out with someone else, and he said there wasn't anyone to go out with. I thought maybe he already had done something with someone else and was feeling guilty. That would explain the 'hurting' part."

"Did you ask him about that?"

"No, not exactly. I didn't think of it at the time. Everything was so rushed on the phone." Then I had a brilliant thought. Why not get Frank's opinion? "You're a guy. What do *you* think he meant?"

"That's hard to say. I do know, though, that if you were *my* girlfriend, I wouldn't do anything to mess that up."

"Now you're kidding again," I said, smiling.

Frank smiled also, but he did not respond.

We were quiet for a few minutes, then Frank said one more thing before Beth and her father returned to the room.

"If you ever want to talk about this some more, I'll be glad to listen. You can call me at school or write if you'd rather. Sometimes it just helps to have someone you can share your thoughts with, and I'll try not to give you my opinion, unless you ask for it, of course."

"Thanks, Frank. I appreciate that." But I had no intention of writing or calling him.

# CHAPTER 21

## "Home for the Holidays"[21]

I had imagined that the three weeks between Thanksgiving and Christmas break would pass quickly, but that was not the case. The days seemed to drag. Although I thought I was prepared to not receive any correspondence from Ned, I still looked for a letter every day. Just habit, I told myself.

On Wednesday morning, the second week back, I couldn't believe my eyes. There it was, sure enough, one lone letter with Ned's familiar writing, sitting in my post office box. I'd recognize that writing anywhere.

"Don't get excited," I warned myself. My heart was pounding. I held the letter in my palm for a moment, fearing that its contents might not be what I hoped for. Tearing the envelope open, I quickly found that my fears were confirmed.

*Dear Annie,*

*I am writing to make sure you understand what I was trying to say on the phone. It's really important to me that you do.*

---

21. "Home for the Holidays"; artist: Perry Como; released 1959.

*You shouldn't keep living your life as if we are a couple. I want you to date other people and not plan a future with me. This will be the best for both of us right now.*

*Love,*
*Ned*

    I should have waited longer to open it and thus prolong my hope. I barely made it back to the room. Sitting on my bed, I read it over and over, feeling the pain a little more each time. He couldn't have been much clearer, I decided. *We're definitely over. I don't have any choice in the matter. He must have found someone else.* Then I became angry. "Damn the stupid war!" I yelled, just about the time that Beth entered the room. That's when the tears began to flow.

    Beth understood immediately, but I handed her the note to answer any questions. She put her arms around me and held me, knowing there was nothing she could say.

    Interestingly, by the next day, I was functioning and, in fact, doing reasonably well. I'm not sure why; possibly, it was a combination of factors. I think I'd known, on some level, that the end was coming, and having it happen actually provided a bit of relief from the anxiety I'd been harboring. Since that which I had most feared had actually occurred, there was little else to worry about. Additionally, I wanted to feel better just to spite him. He wasn't going to have control over my being any longer! On the other hand, it's possible that I never really believed it was truly over, in which case, mourning was unnecessary. At any rate, I went on studying for my pre-holiday tests and planning for Christmas vacation almost like a normal student.

    My normalcy did not go unnoticed. "How are you doing?" Beth asked just two days after the dreaded letter's arrival. We were on our way back to the dorm and had been chatting about her Spanish professor. It was rumored that he'd made suggestive remarks to one of her classmates during a student-teacher conference, and the student hadn't denied those rumors. We were speculating that her silence meant she'd accepted his advances. The student was a somewhat heavy girl and not real attractive with the exception of her long blond hair. The teacher was a middle-aged Hispanic man and, in our minds, also not very appealing. The thought of them together amused us, and we'd been chuckling over that image.

"I don't mean to intrude," Beth continued, "but it seems like you're okay with the latest news from Ned."

"Well, not exactly, but I'm sick of being depressed and really want to get on with my life. As I've said before, if Ned and I were not meant to be, it's better to find that out now. And well, if we *are* meant to be together, then it will happen. I guess it's working because I really do feel okay. I don't think I'm fooling myself."

"I'm glad to hear that," Beth responded. "I was thinking that if you do want to move on, maybe you should make some plans for the holidays. You know Frank is there for you and would probably be interested in more than friendship if you gave him half a chance. Why don't you call him and suggest getting together?"

"Maybe," I said, being as noncommittal as possible. I didn't want to agree to that just yet.

Bleak. That pretty much described the weather when I arrived home for the holidays. I was greeted by gray skies and a bitter chill. "If it's going to be this cold and damp, it might as well snow," my dad announced. Bleak also described my state of mind. It took everything I had to appear cheerful for my parents. I didn't want them worrying about me again.

The highlight of my Christmas turned out to be a phone call from Frank on Christmas Eve.

"I just wanted to wish you happy holidays and let you know that we'll miss you tomorrow at Uncle Bob's and Aunt Ruth's. I'm sure the mashed potatoes won't be the same without your hand in them."

"Oh, I'm sure they'll be just fine," I replied, "but I'll miss being there too. It's going to be pretty quiet at my house."

We reminisced briefly about the great Thanksgiving we'd had, then Frank said, "There's another reason I'm calling."

"What's that?" I inquired.

"One of my fraternity brothers lives in DC. His parents have a huge house in the northwest section. They're quite wealthy. Anyway, he's hosting a big New Year's Eve bash, and I'm invited. Since that's not too far from you, I thought maybe you'd like to go with me. At least I was hoping you would."

This unexpected offer caused my mind to race. Could I come up with a good excuse not to go? *Should* I come up with an excuse? Wouldn't it be better to have something to look forward to other than spending another New Year's Eve at home with my parents? But this would be the beginning of the year I was hoping to see Ned again; should I celebrate that with someone else? *But am I ever going to see Ned again, this year or any year?* I asked myself.

"Annie, are you still there?"

"Uh, yes. I'm here. Just thinking. I don't have any plans, so yes, that sounds like fun." *What am I saying?*

"Good! I'll be there about seven o'clock to pick you up. That will give us time to find his house and arrive by eight. The invitation says semiformal, whatever that means."

"Wow. That means really dressy. I'll have to go shopping."

"Okay. Well, I'll call again to get directions to your house."

"Um, Frank?"

"What, Annie."

"Where will you stay? You don't want to drive all the way back to Petersburg in the middle of the night."

"I don't know. I hadn't thought . . ."

"You could stay here. We don't have a guest room, but I know my parents wouldn't mind if you slept on the couch."

"Are you sure? That would be great!"

"We'll plan on that then. Thanks for the invitation, Frank. And Merry Christmas."

"Merry Christmas to you too, Annie."

*What have I done?* I wondered, hanging up the phone.

"Hey, Annie, come take a look. It's starting to snow!" my father yelled from the front door.

Prospects for a memorable holiday were improving by the minute.

# CHAPTER 22

## "Blue Velvet"[22]

Between shopping for something "semiformal" and working on my art history paper, the week after Christmas went by quickly. On the morning of New Year's Eve, Frank called for directions. "I'm really looking forward to this evening," he said. "It will be great seeing you again."

I was wearing my new blue velvet gown when he arrived just before seven. "Wow! You look fantastic! What a beautiful dress!" he exclaimed.

"You look nice too," I responded. I had never seen him in a suit and tie before, and I was surprised at how handsome he was. His dark brown suit perfectly accentuated his brown hair and brown eyes.

My parents would have been cordial to almost anyone I dated at that point, but they were all over Frank. He had impressed them both. "Have fun and stay out as long as you want," my father called to us as we walked to the car.

"I think they like you," I joked to Frank while he held the car door for me, grateful to be provided with a topic to break the ice. As the evening progressed, I realized that any fears I'd had that our first real date might be a little awkward were unfounded. Frank had a way of putting me completely at ease. I soon learned that others felt that same

---

22. "Blue Velvet"; artist: Bobby Vinton; released 1963.

way about him. Many of his fraternity brothers were at the party, and I could see that they all regarded him as a good friend.

Everything about the gala was elegant, and I was having a surprisingly enjoyable evening. "Huge" was an understatement when describing the house. It was more like a mansion. A band was playing in the "ballroom," where Frank and I were dancing to an old Johnny Mathis song, "Chances Are."

"Just one more hour and we'll be welcoming in the new year," he said, holding me closer. "I'm looking forward to that."

"Yeah, that will be fun," I contributed.

"More than fun. It means I'll get to kiss you," he said, pulling back to observe my reaction.

"Do you need an excuse?" I asked, not to be outdone.

"No, I don't," he replied, continuing to look into my eyes.

In another moment, his lips were on mine, not passionately or with force, just nice and soft. And sweet. He pulled back and looked at me again. And then he kissed me again, this time more passionately. And I kissed him back. Passionately. For several moments, we were lost in the kiss, still swaying to the music. The vocalist was now singing in the background, and I could hear the words "chances are your chances are, awfully good."

As midnight approached, everyone gathered in the ballroom, and the hosts handed out noisemakers and champagne. For the first time that night, I became aware of the glamour surrounding me. I had never seen such beautiful people or gorgeous attire.

Then the countdown began, and suddenly, it was midnight, and Frank was kissing me again. We sang "Auld Lang Syne" and drank our champagne, then began hugging and kissing everyone around us while laughing and blowing our noisemakers. It was the most glorious New Year's celebration I could have ever imagined!

"Thank you for a fabulous evening," I said to Frank a little while later as we were driving home. I was still feeling giddy from the party, not solely from the champagne but from the grand festivities as well. Wanting to prolong that feeling, I scooted over next to Frank and put my head on his shoulder.

"Thank *you* for making it fabulous, Annie," he said, putting his arm around my shoulder and pulling me closer. I felt cozy and comfortable. We drove home like that.

My parents were asleep, or pretending to be, when we got back to my house. They had made up the couch for Frank.

"Let's not chance waking them," Frank insisted. "I want your parents to have a good first impression of me," he said, kissing me on the forehead and sending me to my room.

I lay awake in my bed for a while, replaying it all in my head and basking in the afterglow of a glamorous evening. I realized I had felt happy being there with Frank. And secure. A warm glow embraced me. Was it from the champagne? The party? Or was it Frank?

# 1964

## CHAPTER 23

## "A Hazy Shade of Winter"[23]

"Hi, Roomie. Welcome back. I hear you had quite a time on New Year's Eve."

Beth had returned to campus earlier that day and was sitting on her bed reading when I came in. Apparently, she was anxious to hear about my date with Frank, so I played along. "Just what *did* you hear?"

"I heard that it was an incredible evening and that Frank had a wonderful time."

"Really? What did he say?" Now *I* was curious.

"Let's see. I think his exact words were that it was 'well worth the drive.' I'm anxious to hear your version."

"Yeah, it was a fantastic party—a mansion, glamour, high society. I almost felt like Cinderella."

"Cinderella? So what happened at midnight?"

"We kissed."

"You kissed? How? A real kiss or just a peck? Did you kiss more than once or just at midnight?"

"We kissed ... um ... a few times."

"You did? You made out?"

"Not exactly."

"Annie, tell me!" Beth demanded. "What was it like?"

---

23. "A Hazy Shade of Winter"; artist: Simon & Garfunkel; released 1964.

"We just kissed. It was nice."

"Do you like him?"

"Of course I like him. He's a good friend."

"You know what I mean. Do you *like* him? Are you going out with him again?"

"Yes, well, I don't know. Probably."

"That sounds like a definite maybe," she teased.

"How do I know if he'll even ask me?"

"Of course, he'll ask you! He likes you!"

"How do you know?"

"I just know."

"Well, okay, if he asks me, I'll decide then." Even as I was saying that, I realized that the decision was already made. No question about it. My brief discussion with Beth had brought back the details of that memorable evening and the warm feelings as well. But I wasn't ready to divulge that to her. Nor was I going to let her know that I expected he'd be calling that evening.

After dinner, I returned to the room and half-heartedly opened a book. I was finding it difficult to get back into study mode, and apparently, others were too. Dorm mates were in and out of our room all evening, sharing holiday experiences and catching up on the latest news. Shortly after nine o'clock, Melinda from down the hall knocked on our door, yelling, "Romeo, LD!"

"There he is," Beth said. I was sure she was right; it had to be Frank.

"Hello?" I said, trying not to sound too hopeful.

"Hi, Dear, it's your mom." My heart dropped. She was calling to let me know I'd left several skirts hanging in my closet and that she'd be sending them.

"Okay, thanks, Mom. Got to get back to studying now." Returning to the room, I pretended to Beth that it didn't matter that it wasn't Frank. But even if I didn't admit it to her, I had to admit it to myself. I was definitely disappointed.

Fortunately, I didn't have to wait much longer. Frank called the following evening.

"Hi, Annie, how're you doing? Glad to be back at school?"

"Oh hi, Frank. Yeah, it's great to see everyone again. How about you?"

"Yeah, it's okay. But what would be really great would be to see you. In fact, my friend Stan is coming up there this weekend and offered me a ride. He's even getting a motel room that he said I could share. His girlfriend, Barbara, is a junior there. So how about it?"

"You know exams are coming up."

"I need to study too. We could study together, go to the library or something. It would only be Saturday. We won't be getting there till mid-afternoon. Is it a date then?"

"Okay, I guess. That would be fun. See you then!"

Between my upcoming finals and the cold, damp weather, Frank's visit provided a much-appreciated bright spot in the weekend. We did actually brave the wind and drizzle to make our way to the library, where we found a secluded table in Ringo's beloved "stacks" and managed to put in a good two hours of concentrated study.

Later, after a pleasant dinner with Stan and Barbara at Gino's, a popular date place, which I had never before experienced with a date, Frank and I were sitting in my dorm's parlor. Because I saw him as just a friend, I felt no awkwardness during the silences in our conversation. I didn't think Frank did either. We were comfortable with each other.

"My engineering club throws a big Valentine's shindig every year," Frank said, breaking the silence, "and it's usually a lot of fun. Would you be interested in coming down for it? The party is formal, and there are other events all weekend that are kind of fun too."

Suddenly, I *did* feel awkward.

"Stan says Barbara will be coming. You two could come together," Frank continued, giving me a chance to collect my thoughts before giving him an answer.

The implications of attending this party with Frank were clear. Since this was the event of the year for engineering students, I suspected that their dates were never "just friends." This function was reserved for that special girl—fiancées, steadies, and long-time girlfriends. I didn't fit any of those categories. Yet he was asking me. What did that mean? What would it mean if I said yes?

"It wouldn't have to mean anything," Frank said. *Is he reading my mind?* "Unless you wanted it to."

"What do you mean?" I inquired, speaking finally.

"Oh, Annie. You know us engineering types. We're not so good at expressing our feelings. But it shouldn't be any big secret that I like you. I haven't been out with anyone else since we met. I'd like to think of you as my girlfriend."

"You would?" Now I *really* didn't know what to say.

"Yes, and I'd be proud to have you as my date for the Valentine's dance. What do you think?" He had taken my hand and was holding it in both of his and looking into my eyes. For an engineering guy, he was almost getting romantic.

"I like you too," I stammered.

"Then you'll say yes?"

"Well, okay, yeah, I guess. That sounds like fun."

And then he was kissing me, and his arms were pulling me close to him. His unexpected passion and the softness of his lips caused me to lose myself momentarily. It felt so good. Then I came to.

"Hey, don't forget where we are," I said, pulling away from him and smiling. "Others could be watching."

"Okay, sorry. I got carried away a little. Guess I should be going anyway. Stan said to meet him at his car over by Barbara's dorm. See you in the morning for breakfast about eight o'clock, okay? Stan wants to get an early start back right after that."

He kissed me on the cheek and was gone. I was still standing there watching as he left the dorm.

*\*\*\**

"Sounds like he used the element of surprise on you," Ringo suggested a little later as she and Beth re-lived the evening with me.

"I don't know why you're so surprised," Beth said. "I've always known he likes you."

"It's not just that he likes me," I tried to explain. "It was the way he said it. It was different."

"Different how?" asked Beth.

"Different because it didn't come from Ned," answered Ringo.

"What's that supposed to mean?" I inquired.

"He's the only other guy who's ever said that to you, that's all. So it seemed strange coming from someone new."

Maybe she was right. No one else had ever used those words with me. I was still pondering that thought as I drifted off to sleep.

\*\*\*

I spent semester break, at the end of January, at home disagreeing with my mother over the purchase of a formal. Ruffles have never been my favorite. I'm just not a ruffle person. My mother liked ruffles. "It's not a true formal without them," she said.

And then there was the issue of length. We were in agreement that a short formal somehow seemed less formal, which, from my point of view, was an advantage. My mother, however, felt that if it wasn't to the floor, it wasn't truly a formal. I won out on the length, she on the ruffles. We compromised on a mid-calf-length turquoise taffeta gown, which had a single ruffle down the back, none around the neck, sleeves, or skirt. We were both satisfied.

# CHAPTER 24

## "Save the Last Dance for Me"[24]

The weekend of the dance turned out to be unseasonably cold with a chance of snow. The dreariness of the day, along with the prospect of a long, boring bus ride, almost made me wish I hadn't accepted Frank's invitation. Barbara, on the other hand, couldn't have been more excited.

"This may be a big weekend for us," she began as we settled into our seats on the oversize Greyhound.

"What do you mean?" I asked.

"For Stan and me. I think he's going to pop the question."

"Really?" I wasn't sure what question she meant.

"Yes. He's been acting kind of strange, and I know this sweetheart dance is when a lot of the guys propose to their girlfriends. It's sort of a tradition."

"Oh, I didn't know that," I replied. I didn't even know it was called a sweetheart dance. Frank had neglected to mention that little detail.

"It would be so perfect. If we get engaged now, I'll have plenty of time to plan my wedding. We could have it in June of next year, right after I graduate. I wonder what kind of ring he'll get me."

By the time we arrived in Blacksburg, I had heard all of Barbara's wedding wishes, from the color of her bridesmaids' dresses (peach) to the names of their future children (Mark and Meredith). Frank and

---

24. "Save the Last Dance for Me"; artist: The Drifters; released 1962.

Stan were waiting together for us at the bus station. Frank greeted me with a kiss on the cheek.

"Have a great weekend!" I yelled to Barbara as Frank and I went off to find my bags. Although she and Stan were still involved in their welcoming embrace, she managed to raise her hand and wave in acknowledgment. Since we would not be staying together, I probably wouldn't see her again until the trip back. Frank had arranged a room for me in the home of one of his professors. This was standard practice and allowed for less expensive accommodations. Barbara would be staying at a nearby motel, most likely not alone.

"How was the bus ride?" Frank inquired. If he was just trying to make conversation, he picked a perfect topic.

"It was quite interesting."

"Are you kidding?"

"No, I'm serious," I informed him. "I heard every detail of Barbara's and Stan's wedding plans, even the food they'll serve at the reception."

"Wedding?" Frank exclaimed. "I didn't even know they were engaged!"

"They're not . . . yet. Barbara's hoping he'll ask her this weekend."

"Well, he might. A lot of the guys do that at this dance. That's why it's called the sweetheart dance."

*Now he tells me,* I thought. It was time to change the subject. "I just hope we don't freeze tonight. It sure is cold and dreary." When in doubt, talk about the weather.

***

"What a pretty dress! You look great!" Frank was smiling and seemed excited about our evening together when he picked me up for the dance.

"Thanks. You look good too!" He was wearing a black tux, complete with bow tie and cummerbund. He was definitely a handsome guy.

The elaborate party was held in an armory, which was beautifully decorated. Soft lights had been strung across the ceiling, giving a candle-like glow and providing a mystic atmosphere. In one corner stood an archway, covered with blooming flowers, real ones. Where those had come from I couldn't imagine. Their out-of-place beauty and glorious aroma made it seem that a small slice of paradise had been magically transported to our evening. It was easy to understand why this would be the scene of so many marriage proposals. Photos were being taken under the floral arch so each happy couple could have a lasting keepsake of their special occasion.

I was imagining Barbara and Stan under there and the glowing happiness expressed in their photo, one that they would frame and later show to their children, when Frank surprised me with his suggestion that *we* pose under the arch for a picture. We were slow dancing to the band's rendition of "The Twelfth of Never."

"Us?" I questioned. "Isn't that reserved for . . . you know . . . couples getting engaged?"

"Well, we could pretend just to see how it feels. No one would know the difference. Anyone can get a photo taken there. Since this is my last year here, I'd kind of like to have a memento. Then if things work out for us, we'll have something to look back on and share with our children."

"What?" I exclaimed. "You're kidding, right?" I couldn't tell.

"Not really. I figure the way I feel about you, there's only one way this can go for us."

I couldn't believe what I was hearing. "How *do* you feel about me?" I managed to ask.

"Don't you know? I love you. Why else would I have invited you here tonight? I'm hoping someday you'll be my wife."

There was silence.

"How do *you* feel, Annie?"

*Stunned. Shocked. Flabbergasted.* "Well, I don't know. Surprised, I guess." An understatement.

"You shouldn't be. I feel certain you're the girl for me. Come on, let's do the photo thing."

Standing under the arch with Frank's arm around me, I was able to force a smile. Frank ordered two prints, one for each of us. *A souvenir of me in a daze,* I thought as we returned to the dance floor.

A short time later, I saw Barbara and Stan posing for their picture, both radiant. Her broad smile said it all. It was just as she had hoped. "I am so happy for them," I said to Frank.

\*\*\*

The bus ride back to school was exhilarating, Barbara's enthusiasm being contagious. The time zoomed by as I again heard every detail of their wedding, the reception, and their future life together, this time with the added feature that "Stan agrees with me about this." She was exuberant.

*That's the way it should be,* I thought.

\*\*\*

Despite my initial intentions to not discuss the weekend's events until I had a better grasp on their significance, Beth and Ringo were too persistent to be ignored. I spilled it all to them Sunday evening shortly after my return to campus. Their reactions differed considerably.

"Just think, we could be *family*!" Beth exclaimed after hearing of Frank's remarks. "Our children will be cousins! We—"

"Not so fast!" I interrupted. "Nothing's been decided yet. It was all so sudden."

"How *do* you feel?" Ringo asked, taking a more cautious approach.

"I'm not sure. I like him, but . . ."

"But he's not Ned," Ringo finished the thought for me.

"Yes, and well, there's more to it than that. His comments were so matter-of-fact. It just wasn't romantic."

"What happened afterwards?" Beth inquired. "What did you do after the dance?"

"We went with his friend Fred and his date, Joan, to a little coffee shop called "The Cellar," where they had a jazz band. Lots of the couples went there. It's kind of a local hangout. We were there till nearly two in the morning. Then he took me back to Dr. Blair's house, where I was staying."

"And then?" asked Beth. "Did he come in with you? Did you make out or what?"

"No, you nosy girl. He wasn't allowed to come to my room. We stood on the porch for a few minutes, but it was freezing. He kissed me a couple of times. Then he left."

"That's it?" they both inquired.

"Yup, that's it. Nothing juicy to report."

***

The subject didn't come up again for several months, either with my dorm friends or with Frank. Everything went along as if it had NEVER come up, so much so that I began to wonder if I had imagined the whole scenario.

# CHAPTER 25

## "Did You Ever Have to Make Up Your Mind?"[25]

End-of-year exams were nearly on us again, and Ringo was dragging me to the library for some quiet study time.

"What's new with Frank?" she inquired as we made our way across campus. "You two seem to be an item." Although Ringo always went right to the point, I usually didn't feel like she was prying but rather that she was asking because she truly cared about me, making it easy to be straight with her.

"The truth is, I'm not sure," I replied, searching my mind for the best way to describe Frank's and my relationship. "It's true we've seen each other almost every weekend this spring, but nothing serious has happened. We mostly just hang out, see a movie or something. Often with some of his friends."

"No more proposals?"

"No. It wasn't ever that anyway. You know, he kids around a lot, so when he does imply something, I'm never sure how serious he is."

"Well, you know the old saying, 'the truest words are said in jest.' I think he uses his joking to hide behind because he's afraid to tell you how he really feels."

---

25. "Did You Ever Have to Make up Your Mind?"; artist: The Lovin' Spoonful; released 1965.

"I've thought of that. But I'm not sure. And it doesn't matter anyway. We just have a good time together, and that's all I want for now."

"And what about Ned?" I should have seen that coming, but it caught me off guard. I was quiet for a minute.

"Oh, I don't know. Of course, I think about him. He was my first love. And I wonder if he's okay and all. I guess I'd really like to hear from him to know that he's all right."

"And that's all?"

"I don't know. I need to think about that."

So that's exactly what I did when I got to the library. After convincing Ringo that we should go our separate ways, I found a secluded table on the second floor. I knew that Ringo would opt for the basement and her much-loved stacks. I opened my probability and statistics notebook and set it aside. Buried beneath the many paper fragments I had stuffed in my wallet was a well-worn photo of Ned. Carefully extracting it, I set it on the table in front of me. Funny how the twinkle in his eye was captured in the picture. *Now I'm going to be objective,* I told myself. I reminisced about our early times together and how openly I had loved him. And he me. Then I thought about his leaving, and now not hearing from him at all. *Is he even alive?* How confusing it all was. *If I find out he's okay and hasn't let me know, that's a pretty definite sign that he no longer cares about me,* I concluded. My warm thoughts of the past were being replaced with feelings of hurt and anger. *It's just not fair,* I said almost out loud as I felt the old familiar stinging sensation developing in my eyes. *I'm not going to cry.* Determined to not feel sorry for myself any more, I reached back into my wallet and quickly found Frank's photo, which wasn't buried at all but in clear view. I set it next to Ned's. I stared at them both for a short time. How different they were and how different my feelings for them were. It slowly became clear to me that Frank was the one who was now there for me. He had patiently stood by and waited when I pined over Ned. Like a rock, he was someone I could depend on. How secure life would be with him, knowing I could always count on his strength. Something clicked within me then, and I felt that a weight had been lifted from my shoulders. I *could* be free to care about Frank, and why not do it? He was reality; Ned was a dream from the past. "Yes!" I wanted to scream.

Gathering my stuff, I jumped up and ran down the two flights of stairs to find Ringo. She was in her usual spot, the far corner of the stacks, hunched over her English lit book. "C'mon!" I yelled in a not-so-quiet whisper. "Let's go get a soda. I need to talk."

\*\*\*

"So that was my thought process while I was in the library," I explained to her a few minutes later as we sipped on Cokes in the campus snack bar. "One of them is choosing to be here for me, and the other has chosen not to. It's obvious which one really cares about me. 'Actions speak louder than words,' as they say."

"Are you saying you don't love Ned anymore?"

Ah, Ringo, always straight to the point. "I keep asking myself that question, and this is what I've come up with: In some ways, I'll always love him. Or at least the person he used to be. But I don't even know who he is now, so how can I love him?"

"And do you love Frank?" I should have known that would be next.

"He's so sweet and caring. I really like him a lot."

"That wasn't the question."

"I think I *could* love him . . ."

"But you're not in love with him?"

"Oh, Ringo, it's so hard to put into words. We get along well, and I always enjoy being with him. I could see us many years down the road, raising our kids together and enjoying wonderful family Thanksgiving feasts with all the Reynolds clan."

"Well, if you won't discuss the L- word, then what about the S-word? How about sex with him?" she continued to probe. "Have you guys even talked about doing 'it'?"

"Actually, yes, we have talked about it. He says that he wants to wait until he's at least engaged before he asks a girl to do that with him. And I said I agreed."

"Miss Virginity, eh? Were you pretending that you'd never done it with Ned?"

"No, he never asked."

"Or that he'd never done it with Janice?" she persisted.

"I didn't ask either. It's not important."

"It might be important if they *didn't* do it," Ringo said. "It just doesn't seem normal somehow, a healthy guy like him not wanting to have sex. Maybe there's a problem."

Now she'd gone too far, and I was on the defensive. "I think it's refreshing, finally someone who's not just out to see how far he can go. It's one of the things I like about him. There's nothing wrong with that!"

"Sorry. Didn't mean to upset you," she apologized. "Just had to make sure. Sounds like perhaps he *is* one of the rare good guys, so maybe you should go for it with him."

"That's kind of what I was thinking. Thanks."

\*\*\*

I lay awake for hours that night, contemplating what life with Frank might be like. It seemed quite attractive. *He's loyal, smart, thoughtful, and funny, and he'd certainly father some great-looking kids.* I stopped there, trying to imagine what kind of daddy he'd make. Pretty good, I decided. I'd seen him with Beth's brother, Chip. They were great buddies. No problems in that area or any other area that I could come up with. Did I have the perfect potential mate right under my nose? It definitely seemed so. Pondering those thoughts, I finally drifted off to sleep.

After this new revelation, Frank's comment on the phone the next evening was a bit freaky, or was it fate?

\*\*\*

"Hi, Annie," he started out. "How's my favorite math whiz?"

"Oh hi, Frank. I'm fine. What's up with you?" I noticed I was making a forced effort at sounding casual, not yet ready to disclose my newfound realizations about "us" with him. He apparently was more concerned with his own agenda and didn't notice the strain in my voice.

"Funny you should ask," he replied. "I was thinking I'd like to come up this weekend and spend some time alone with you. There are a couple of things we need to discuss. Maybe we could go out to dinner Saturday night, just the two of us?"

"Okay, sure. That would be fun." *What on earth is he talking about?*

"It's a date."

"Yes, it is. I'll be there mid-afternoon, around three o'clock. See you then."

Although I didn't share the content of our brief conversation with either Beth or Ringo, Frank's words replayed themselves in my mind all week, "a couple of things we need to discuss, just the two of us." *What does that mean? Is something big about to happen?*

# CHAPTER 26

## "You Don't Have to Say You Love Me"[26]

The first surprise of the evening was that Frank had made dinner reservations for us at the George Washington Inn. Going there for anything other than watching the wealthy socialites spend their money had never even been an option before. He definitely had something unusual in mind.

"What will I wear?" was my initial reaction when he shared his plan.

"You always look nice. I'm sure you'll find something," he offered in an unsuccessful attempt at being helpful. "I brought my charcoal gray suit, so any of your dresses would be fine."

Frank apparently had never noticed that, aside from the two dances we had attended, the only dress he'd ever seen me wear was my blue and white pinstripe Villager shirtwaist. That would hardly work on this occasion, but I knew right where to go for something more appropriate. My suitemate Laney had a much more stylish wardrobe and a vast selection from which to choose. Fortunately, we wore the same size. With her help, and input from both Beth and Ringo, I decided on her two-piece powder blue wool blend dress. It was just classy enough. I allowed Beth to put my hair in a French twist, and then she insisted

---

26. "You Don't Have to Say You Love Me"; artist: Dusty Springfield; released 1966.

on doing my makeup. In the end, I looked stunning, quite a change from my usual casual self. The downside was that now each of my three fashion consultants had her own suspicions of what the evening had in store.

"I'm thinking it might be a special night," Beth said, and their eyes all shared a knowing agreement.

"Wow! You look beautiful!" Frank exclaimed as I entered the dorm's parlor, where he was waiting patiently. He had never before said I was beautiful. The night had already become special.

"You look pretty good yourself," I managed to reply as Frank stood up and kissed me on the cheek.

Dinner went less awkwardly than it could have. We had filet mignon, baked potatoes, and salad. Frank had a glass of red wine. We managed to make small talk throughout the meal, and more remarkably, neither of us made any social faux pas, or at least none that caused any noticeable stares from other patrons. Finally, over chocolate mousse, Frank said, "Annie, we need to talk."

"Okay," I said.

"Annie," he continued as if he had memorized a speech, "you know I'll be graduating soon."

"Uh-huh . . ."

"And I'll be getting a job."

"Yes . . ."

"The thing is, I don't want to have to move away. I mean away from you. And here's the other thing. I've been offered a job near here, right up the road in Prince William County. It's with the Army Corps of Engineers. They're going to build a new water treatment plant just outside of Quantico. The pay is good, it would be great experience, and I could be near you. Also, because it's a 'critical occupation,' it will exempt me from being drafted and possibly going to war. This is important because I will lose my 'II S' student deferment as soon as I graduate."

"That's a relief," I said. I couldn't imagine sending another boyfriend off to war. I just couldn't go through that again.

"They want me to start right after graduation," he continued. Then he paused for a moment and looked right at me. He reached up and rested his hand on mine. *Here it comes,* I thought. "And well, Annie, how would you feel about that?"

"Uh, well, that would be fine. But it's not up to me."

"Well, here's another thing. I have a second offer. It's very similar and just as good financially. But it's a little farther away, in Texas."

"Oh!"

"So what do you think?"

"Um, well, what do *you* want to do?" I was thrown completely off balance and didn't know what to say. This wasn't going at all as I had envisioned.

"I already told you that I don't want to leave you. I'd rather take the job here and keep seeing you. I could even get a place right here near the college, if you agree."

"Sure, that would be great."

"Then when we get married, you could just move right in."

"What?" Now he had my full attention. "What do you mean?"

"I mean I want us to get married . . . someday."

"Frank, uh, I don't know what to say."

"Don't say anything right now. Just think about it. If we were married and living here, you could still finish school while I work at Quantico."

"I'd be a Townie!" The idea made me laugh. "But what's the hurry? We don't have to be married to see each other. We could still date and do things on weekends and stuff."

"Well, how about if we get engaged? Then I'll know you're mine, and I'll accept the job offer."

Something about his proposal didn't feel right. "This is all so sudden. And it's almost time for me to be back. Let's call it a night, okay?"

"As long as you promise to think about this. It means a lot to me."

"Okay, I promise." *How can I NOT think about it?*

\*\*\*

Ringo was the only one still awake when I returned to the dorm. She wanted to know everything.

"What happened? What did he say? Did you tell him how you feel?"

"I'm not sure what happened. It's all so confusing." I ended up telling her everything.

"So let me get this straight," she said when I was done. "He actually *did* ask you to marry him but without getting down on his knee, looking into your eyes, and declaring his everlasting love." She had hit the nail on the head.

"Yeah, it was just so matter-of-fact."

"Well, in case you haven't noticed," Ringo said, "Frank is a matter-of-fact kind of guy. It doesn't mean he loves you any less. In fact, he's probably a lot more loyal and dependable than someone who might be more exciting. There's something to be said for that. You'll always be able to believe what he says. The real question is 'How do *you* feel?'"

I knew that was coming.

"Here's the thing. I *did* want him to say those things. I just wanted him to say them differently. I guess it doesn't change how I feel though. I am so comfortable around him, and he makes me feel safe. With him, I don't have to worry about being hurt again. I know I don't want to lose him. And I definitely don't want him moving to Texas! I couldn't handle another long-distance relationship."

"Good. That settles it then. Now let's get some sleep."

"Thanks for your help." It may have been settled in her mind; I still wasn't sure.

# CHAPTER 27

## "Graduation Day"[27]

Frank's graduation was two weeks later. School was out for the summer, and I was back home, so I took the bus from DC all the way to Blacksburg, alone. A very long trip. Graduation was hot and, for the most part, boring. Beth and her parents were there, as well as Frank's parents and grandparents, making it a bit more tolerable. Beth and I sat together, whispering and giggling. Afterwards, we all went out for a celebratory dinner, and I again found myself in the middle of the "all American family," right out of central casting.

"Frank, my boy, you thought college was hard. Just wait till you experience the *real* world," Beth's father was the first to speak.

"He's right, son. No more partying all night and sleeping all day," Frank's father joined in.

"Yeah, I did a lot of that," Frank said, playing along with their good-natured teasing.

Inevitably, the conversation soon turned to me. It was Frank's sweet grandma who began. "Annie, dear, I'm sure you're looking forward to having Frank so close by," she said. "No more of those long rides back and forth. What do you call them . . . street trips?"

"Road trips, Grandma," Frank corrected gently.

---

27. "Graduation Day"; artist: The Beach Boys; released 1966.

"That's nice, Dear. And I'll bet real soon, there'll be a ring on Annie's finger, and we'll be planning a wedding." *Funny how people over sixty can get away with saying whatever's on their mind and no one seems to care,* I thought.

"Not so fast, Grandma," Frank responded quickly, feeling the sudden heat. "One step at a time," he added, noticing my panicked expression.

"What's great is that he's found a good job so quickly. Many of his classmates don't even know what they're going to do next," I said. My attempt to divert the attention away from "us."

"Certainly something to be proud of," Frank's father said, following my lead. "What exactly will you be doing? Do you know yet?"

"I think I'm in charge of all the Marines at Quantico," Frank joked, "keeping them in line when they date those college girls." I breathed a sigh of relief as Frank went on to provide his understanding of the job description. *What a perfect family this would be to marry into,* I couldn't help thinking. *They really care about one another. And they care about me too.*

"Where will you be living, Dear?"

"Actually, Grandma, I have some news about that, which I haven't shared with anyone yet, not even Annie. I was looking for a place to rent and came across this little house just a few blocks from the college campus, right there on Franklin Street. I was all set to sign a year's lease on it when the couple decided to sell. He's being shipped overseas, and she's going to move back home somewhere. Rhode Island, I think. Anyway, the price was right, and I put a down payment on it." Frank was looking at me, not his grandma, as he spoke.

"Well, that's right nice, Dear," she replied, oblivious to the fact that he was not directing his words at her.

"You're not kidding?" I asked, forcing myself out of my stunned silence.

"No, I'm serious. I'm a homeowner! What do you think?"

"That's good, I guess. I'm just, uh, surprised."

"Well, I think it's great!" his dad exclaimed, diverting the attention again. "My son's all grown up, graduating from college, getting a job, and buying a house! This deserves a toast," he continued, reaching for his iced tea. "Here's to your many accomplishments. Your mom and I are proud of you."

"Hear, hear," everyone chimed in, sanctifying the toast with the clinking of our glasses.

We were all staying at a nearby motel that night. Beth and I were sharing a room, once again. I wasn't sure if she'd mind my asking Frank to come in and talk for a while, so I was relieved when she was the one who extended the invitation.

"We can have our own celebration, just the three of us. Wait till you see what I have in my suitcase," she said as Frank was shutting the door behind him.

She dug down through a few layers of clothing and pulled out two bottles. "Champagne!" she announced.

"Where did you get *that*?" Frank demanded.

"From Mom and Dad. They'll never miss it. They keep several bottles on hand for special occasions. This is a pretty special occasion, don't you think?"

"All right, but I don't want to be responsible for getting you girls in trouble."

"It's okay. We'll just have a few sips," Beth explained. "Here, you pop it," she said, handing one of the bottles to Frank.

He obeyed, shooting the top across the room. Beth was waiting with three plastic cups, which they proceeded to fill.

"Here's to my favorite cousin and to my best friend," Beth toasted, along with the silent clink of our plastic ware. We all took a sip.

Frank followed with a toast of his own. "And here's to *my* favorite cousin for coming up with this idea and to *my* best friend, Annie, the sweetest girl in the whole world." We had another sip.

I knew it was my turn. Thinking quickly, I raised my cup again. "And here's to two of the most wonderful friends a person could ever wish for," I offered as we took another sip.

Then Frank started again. "Here's to our mutual admiration society. May it long endure."

"To endurance!" Beth and I exclaimed in unison, causing us both to break out in giggles.

And so it went, with us getting sillier and sillier. A few rounds later, Beth's looseness caused me to sober up a bit. "Here's to the two of you getting married," she blurted out. "We'll all be family then! Here's to raising our children together," she continued. "And here's to little Franks and little Annies coming to my house for Thanksgiving!" There was no stopping her.

"Here's to the future, whatever it brings," I said finally, trying to get her off that track.

"The future nothing. I'm talking about this summer. I want to be a bridesmaid in your wedding this summer." I had never seen Beth drink like this before, and I didn't like it.

"We're not planning a summer wedding," I said stiffly.

"Well, you better, if you want to see each other in the fall when we're back in school."

"What are you talking about?" I demanded.

"You know the rules, Roomie. You know we're not allowed to date Townies."

"Oh my god, she's right," I stammered, letting the truth of her words seep through the bubbles and into my brain. "I'd forgotten that. What are we going to do?"

"I guess we'll be getting married," Frank said, setting his cup down and coming towards me. "It's what I want, and if you want it too, why not?" He put both arms around me and looked down into my eyes. "Annie, will you marry me? Right now? This summer?"

*What is happening here?* I thought. I tried to shake the fog out of my brain. "I don't know, I guess," I responded finally. "We may just have to get married, I suppose."

Resting my head on his chest, I allowed myself to melt into the security of his embrace.

# CHAPTER 28

## "I Can See Clearly Now"[28]

Despite the alcohol I'd consumed, I didn't sleep well that night. Frank had fallen asleep on my bed, fully clothed, and I lay there next to him, troubled by the revelation of the night before. *Should we get married? Is this the first night of a lifetime of sleeping next to Frank?* If I didn't marry him, what would happen? Turning down his proposal would essentially involve breaking up with him since I wouldn't legally be able to see him anymore. The one thing I was sure of was that I didn't want that. He was my support, my security, my rock. Not seeing him anymore would put me back in that scary undefined place of not knowing where I was going. I briefly considered the idea of staying in the dorm and seeing him on the sly but quickly dismissed it. Aside from that night with Ned, and one time when I got in trouble for not wearing my freshman beanie, I had not broken any college rules. Breaking one on a continuing basis was simply not an option.

By morning, I was planning my life as Frank's wife. *Frank's wife.* I said it to myself several times to let it sink in. It would be a great life, I decided. Spending Thanksgivings and Christmases with the Reynolds bunch. Maybe even Easters and summer vacations. Our children growing up with Beth's children. *Children.* How many would we have? I could easily imagine Frank as a daddy; he was so patient and level

---

28. "I Can See Clearly Now"; artist: Johnny Nash; released 1970.

headed. Naturally, I would stay home to raise our kids. I knew Frank would agree to that. His mother, Beth's mother, and mine had all been stay-at-home moms. *Frank's salary as an engineer will easily support us if I postpone a career to be with the children, at least while they're little,* I reasoned. *What a perfect life it will be,* I concluded.

"Good morning. How's my future bride?" Frank had rolled over and propped himself up on his elbow.

"Good morning," I replied. *Bride?* I hadn't even considered a wedding! "I'm fine. Just lying here, wondering if last night really happened."

"Oh, it happened all right. You agreed to marry me."

"Yes, I remember. I wasn't sure if *you* would. Or if it was just the alcohol talking."

"No, silly. I was serious. I hope *you* were. I *wasn't* drunk, you know."

"And I remember too!" Beth had awakened and joined in the discussion from the bed next to ours. "You guys are getting married . . . you guys are getting married . . .," she began in a sing song chant. "Let's go tell the family!"

So Beth announced our news to the family in the middle of breakfast in the motel restaurant. They were not surprised. I guess they all figured it was a done deal way before I did. Their concern was the wedding.

"Of course you'll get married in our church, the one you grew up in," his grandmother stated. "I can talk to the pastor right away, and we'll set the date."

"Then there'll be lists of guests and invitations and finding a place for the reception and rehearsal dinner . . . and . . .," Frank's mother said. "We can start on all that tomorrow."

"Mom, Annie hasn't even told her parents yet. They might have something to say about it," Frank reminded her.

"We don't have much time," she continued. "I'm sure they'll appreciate our help."

"I'm sure they will," I said. "We'll have to get everyone together to discuss the plans." I realized my parents hadn't even met Frank's family. I had no doubt, though, that they would like them just as much as I did.

"Why don't I come home with you to break the news to them?" Frank offered. "I don't have to report to work till the end of the week. I could drive you home tomorrow, unless you're counting on another exciting bus ride, that is," he teased.

"I think I can forgo the bus ride," I responded. "Sounds like a plan!"

My parents were a bit surprised by our news but happy for us nonetheless.

"Of course you'll get married in our church, the one you grew up in," my mother voiced after allowing the idea of a wedding to digest. "We can talk to our pastor right away to set the date." *Where have I heard that before?* Frank and I shared a concerned glance, realizing that this wasn't going to be as easy as we'd hoped.

Later that night, Frank and I confronted the issue.

"I was hoping it would all fall into place," he said. "But it looks like we're dealing with some conflicting wishes about our wedding ceremony. The important thing, though, is what *you* want to do. What are *your* thoughts?"

"We're certainly not going to be able to please everybody. Here's an idea: how about we don't please any of them?"

"And do *what*?" Frank asked, startled.

"Well, this is just a thought, and you may not like it. But it would save all the hassle of planning a big wedding."

"You want to elope?" he asked. "That's fine with me!"

"No, that's not what I meant."

"Then what?"

"You know my favorite math professor, Dr. Roberts? He's also a minister at a local church near the college. I've been to his services a few times. He's actually performed marriages for several of the students. I'm thinking that if we could get him to do it, we could have a small family wedding right there in Martinsburg, our new hometown! That way, neither set of parents would feel like the other side was getting their way. They'd all be equally slighted. Maybe we could do it in mid-August, right before school starts. I'd really like to have Ringo there."

"That's a great idea, Annie!"

And so it was. Before saying anything to the families, we decided to pay a visit to Dr. Roberts, which we did the following day. He agreed enthusiastically, and we set the date for the Saturday before classes were to resume.

"This is perfect," I said to Frank.

"Yes, it is."

My parents were less than thrilled when we broke the news to them, but they soon came around. They even offered to give us the money that they would have spent on a large wedding. "You're saving us a bundle," my dad said. "You might as well have it to buy furniture or whatever else you need for your new house."

"That's very generous of you, Mr. Barstow," Frank said. "We really appreciate it."

"You're welcome. And by the way," he continued, "you're going to have to stop being so formal. You can call us 'Mom' and 'Dad,' if you want, or even 'Kathryn' and 'Harold,' if that's more comfortable for you." I knew they really liked Frank, much more than they would ever express to me.

"Thanks, uh, Dad," Frank said.

Frank left the next day with the promise to return on Friday after work. That night, I called Ringo.

"Hi, Roomie. What's up?"

"You're not gonna believe this," I told her. "I have some news."

"Well, spill it!"

"Are you sitting down?" I asked.

"Yes, I'm sitting. What is it? Did you hear from Ned?"

*Oh my god. Why did she say that?* I froze, astounded by her question.

"Annie, are you there? What's your news?"

I regained my composure. "My news is that Frank and I are getting married. In August, before school starts."

"Really?"

"Really. We just decided."

"That's great! Tell me how it happened."

I related the whole story, including every detail. "And that's where we are," I concluded. "Can you be there?"

"Of course. I wouldn't miss it. I'll be there . . ." She paused and then added, "if you're sure that's what you truly want."

"Yes, I'm sure."

"Annie, can I ask you something?"

"Nothing's ever stopped you before. Shoot."

"Are you happy?"

"Of course I am. I wouldn't do this if I weren't. Don't you know that?"

"There's just something . . . I can't quite put my finger on it. Like you didn't make this decision. It was made for you or something."

"Then it's fate! Who am I to argue with that?"

"How about the sex thing? Have you talked about it yet? Or have you maybe already done it?"

"No, it hasn't come up. We'll have plenty of time for that after the wedding."

"Okay, one more question. Then I'll let you go. Is he giving you an engagement ring?"

"Uh, I don't know. I haven't thought about it. Maybe he's going to surprise me with one. And if he doesn't, that's okay. Our engagement isn't going to be very long anyway. Pretty soon, I'll be wearing a wedding ring, and he will too!"

She still wasn't satisfied. "This is a big step you're taking. I just hope it's for the right reasons. You've always talked about doing things the traditional way, wearing a diamond solitaire engagement ring, planning a big wedding with lots of bridesmaids, having your father walk you down the aisle in front of all your friends and relatives. Those things have always been important to you. Are you sure you want to give up on all your dreams?"

"My real dream is having a happy, secure marriage, and that's what I'm planning on." She was almost starting to irritate me.

"Don't be upset. I only want what's best for you. It's just that, well, uh, I don't know."

"What?"

"You don't sound very excited or something . . ."

"I *am* excited. I'm excited that I'm not going to let another opportunity for happiness slip by like I did when Ned wanted me to marry him and I thought we should wait. I'm not making that mistake again. What is that saying? Seize the day? Or as my sweet Grammy would advise, 'make hay while the sun shines.'"

"Okay, it sounds like you know what you're doing, and that's all I care about. You and Frank have my congratulations."

"Thanks, Ringo. That means a lot."

# CHAPTER 29

# "Going to the Chapel"[29]

I was working in DC again that summer, this time for the Daughters of the American Revolution (DAR). A friend of my mother had notified us of the opportunity, and I was selected for the position based solely on my penmanship. Nine other college girls and I had been hired to transcribe, by hand, the lists of DAR members from one ledger to another, state by state. The work was tedious and would have been unbearable had it not been for the camaraderie that quickly developed among the workers, not unlike that of any group of individuals held captive for any length of time. We laughed so much that the administrator in charge finally separated us. Even so, we still found ways to pass notes back and forth, stopping by one another's desks on the way to or from the restroom, and thus keep ourselves entertained. The work itself was undemanding, requiring little more than decent eyesight and clear handwriting, which left my mind free to ponder my upcoming wedding.

Because we had chosen to forgo an elaborate ceremony, my biggest decision was what I should wear. My mother and I finally agreed that a knee-length dress—in white, of course—dressy but not formal, would be most appropriate. Finding the perfect one, however, was not so easy. We spent hours pursuing white summer dresses, rummaging through every clothing store in town. We even crossed the bridge into DC one

---

29. "Going to the Chapel"; artist: The Dixie Cups; released 1964.

Saturday morning to check out Woodward and Lothrop. Ultimately, we found the ideal candidate on a sale rack in J. C. Penney. Known for her frugality, my mother was elated. I too was pleased with the choice despite its discounted price tag. Much of the dress's appeal was in its simplicity, a fitted sleeveless version in pure white polished cotton. The matching jacket had three-quarter-length sleeves and was decorated in brocade. And, we found a coordinating pillbox hat with a short veil in the bridal shop, also on sale. White pumps completed the outfit. I would carry a bouquet of my favorite flower, carnations, in pink and white, and Frank would wear a single white carnation as his boutonniere.

The "reception," to be held in the church hall, would be handled by the church ladies and would consist of punch and finger sandwiches, along with a small wedding cake that they would provide. Our photographer was to be Henry, an older gentleman whom I had met in photography class two years before. He had expanded his hobby into a small business. The guest list consisted of immediate family members and a few close friends on each side. Beth would be my attendant, and her brother, Chip, would be Frank's. The wedding plans were complete.

Of more concern to me that summer was life following the wedding. Not being in the dorm would be a big adjustment, not to mention the idea of trying to keep house while going to school. It had been difficult enough just accomplishing my laundry once a week; now I was going to have to dust, vacuum, grocery shop, prepare meals, and scrub floors as well. My cooking skills were nonexistent, and the cleaning ones weren't much better. The biggest challenge to my DAR job that summer was keeping my mind from dwelling on those thoughts. *Many other brides have survived with no prior experience, and I can too,* I told myself. *It will be just like playing house!*

Beth was phoning me every other day, it seemed, to re-confirm the wedding plans, and especially her role, in my big day.

"I'm your only attendant, and I want to get it right," she would repeat each time. Of course, we were both excited that we'd soon be "related," even if it was only by marriage. "We'll be in-laws of some sort," she'd reaffirm often.

"Well, that's better than outlaws, as Frank would say," I'd usually reply.

I even shared with her my concerns about being able to stay on top of the housework. She pointed out that "Ringo's friend Tina seems to be handling it all okay, so I have no doubts that you can too," which was somewhat reassuring.

About a month before the big day, I had a call from Ringo. She began by asking about the wedding plans, which I described in great detail.

"You're definitely coming, aren't you?" I inquired. "And bringing Danny?"

"Oh yes, we'll be there." Then, just as I had suspected, it became clear that she had more than just the actual ceremony on her mind. "And how are you feeling about it all?" she asked.

*Uh-oh, here it comes,* I thought. "I'm feeling fine. Everything seems to be falling into place."

"You know that's not what I mean."

"Well, if you're asking if I'm having doubts or second thoughts, I'm not. I truly feel I'm doing the right thing. I just don't understand why you keep asking."

"The truth is, I'm a little concerned that you don't use the L-word very often when it comes to Frank. It makes me wonder if you're really in love with him."

"Of course I love him. I wouldn't be marrying him if I didn't, and I have to say, I find it insulting that you keep questioning me." I couldn't help feeling defensive, and I didn't like the feeling. "Frank and I are a good match. You'll see," I continued, more determined than ever to prove to her that ours would be a lasting union.

"Okay, okay, I'm sorry. Just playing the devil's advocate, as they say. You know I love you and wish you the best. If you say you're happy, I believe you. Danny and I will be there with bells on!"

"All right. See you then." *Maybe she's just envious because I'm having Beth as my attendant and not her,* I thought as we hung up the phone.

\*\*\*

Frank was settling into his job and actually loving it. The work was challenging yet not stressful to him. And he kept regular hours, from eight thirty in the morning to five o'clock in the afternoon, with few demands for weekends or overtime. He came to see me every weekend, and he seemed really happy about our upcoming nuptials.

"It will be so great to have you there, Annie, to come home to every evening. And you know, with you being in school full time, I'll be able to help with all the stuff around the house. I've been doing my own laundry for years, so I won't mind doing yours too. I'm not much of a cook, but I sure can wash dishes. And with a little training, I might even be capable of dusting and vacuuming."

His words served to ease my worries over the housekeeping responsibilities. "You're just too good to be true," I said after a moment of contemplation. "How did I get to be so lucky?"

"And all this time I thought *I* was the lucky one," he responded, taking my hand. "It's nice to know the feeling's mutual. I guess we're both lucky." And then he kissed me.

I had just gained an increased appreciation for the kind and gentle man who was soon to be my husband.

# CHAPTER 30

## "With This Ring"[30]

It rained on our wedding day. Although I laughed it off to everyone, adamantly denying that a little precipitation could possibly have any connection to our future wedded bliss, I secretly had my doubts. A little "worry" demon residing just beyond my carefree facade kept bringing up the possibility that the inclement weather was indeed a bad omen. But even if I had consciously acknowledged this concern, I don't think I would have acted on it or done anything differently. Plans had progressed way too far. Our family and friends had all gathered for the happy occasion, and I was not one to rock the boat at that point. Any uneasiness I might have been feeling would remain suppressed. When I declared, "I, Annie, take thee, Frank," I sincerely believed we were following our true paths. A calm fell over me, a peacefulness I had never before experienced.

Twenty-one of our relatives and friends had assembled for the celebration. The relatives were mostly Frank's; the friends mostly mine. He had invited one new acquaintance from work, a charming single guy named Michael, who proved to be fair game for the six unattached MWC ladies in attendance. Frank, Beth, Ringo, and I spent the reception as it were (offering only finger sandwiches, wedding

---

30. "With This Ring"; artist: The Platters; released 1967.

cake, and nonalcoholic punch), speculating on which one of the flock Michael would end up with.

"Don't worry, he's a decent guy," Frank whispered to me at one point. "He'll only date one of them at a time."

All the male guests, except for Danny, offered toasts, beginning with Chip, whose short presentation was obviously done out of duty as the best man. "To my new cousin-in-law and my old cousin."

Frank's dad and Beth's dad both followed, making similar long-winded statements about how I had always been a part of their family, and now it was official. Frank's grandpa chimed in with his agreement. Not to be outdone, my father was next. "Marriage is an honorable institution," he said. "Every family should have one." *How embarrassing,* I thought. *What does that even mean?* My parents were just not socially adept.

Michael then surprised us all by offering his comments. "So what's up for the honeymoon? Besides *that*, I mean," he added, laughing. "Where are you guys going?"

"Since I have to be back at work on Tuesday, we're just going over to Colonial Beach for two nights," Frank announced to everyone in a tone that came across as somewhat apologetic. "We have the honeymoon suite in their best hotel, and we'll be dining at the yacht club." Colonial Beach was located on the Potomac River, about an hour's drive east of Martinsburg. It was by no means a fancy resort, as I'm sure all our guests were well aware. I had enjoyed many memorable trips there with my parents in my younger years when there was little money for such extravagances as a real vacation.

"It doesn't matter where you go," Michael piped up again. "You won't be seeing much of the out-of-doors anyway. And I'm sure you'll rise to the occasion."

"I'll drink to that!" Frank's father proposed as the men all chuckled and held up their glasses.

My worry demon nudged me again as I couldn't help but wonder if their implication of a highly sensual weekend would prove correct. Sex with Frank was still a big unknown.

We were soon hugging our goodbyes in preparation for our departure.

"I'm so happy," I whispered to Ringo as we embraced tightly. "This feels right."

"Good. I'm happy for you," she replied, giving me an extra squeeze and a kiss on the cheek.

What followed then was the only aspect of our day that might be considered traditional. Ours was the classic exit scene, Frank and I ducking the rice shower and hurrying to get into his car, stopping only to pose for one final photo to complete the album documenting Our Wedding Day.

# 2011

## IN THE CABIN

"Oh, Tulip," Annie said. "I've been neglecting you, you poor sweet girl. I'll take a break now so we can go outside. Oh wait, there's the phone . . . You go ahead," she said, opening the cabin door.

"Ringo!"

"Hi, Annie."

"Oh my gosh. I never returned your call! I'm so sorry. I've been engrossed in the past, trying to figure out how I got where I am today and what I might do differently if I had it to do over."

"That's profound. What have you decided?"

"Nothing yet. Just mostly reminiscing. We sure had some crazy times at MWC."

"Yeah, we did. Seems like several lifetimes ago. And now everything's changed. They actually have *male* students! Can you imagine what that would have been like for us, having boys in our classes? We wouldn't have gotten any work done! And it's no longer just a college. It's the *University* of Martinsburg!"

"That's weird, huh? So what's new with you guys, and why the call?"

"Danny and I are planning a little getaway in our RV next week, and we thought if you're going to be around, we might stop by for a visit."

"That would be wonderful! I'd love to see you both. I plan to be up here at the cabin for another week or so. You could come here! How long can you stay?"

"We don't have any schedule, at least not yet. Maybe we should come there first . . . How about this Saturday?"

"Perfect."

"What can we bring?"

"Just your sweet selves. I'll be going shopping in Waynesboro tomorrow, so I'll get lots of food and plenty of rocky road ice cream, just like old times! Hope Danny can put up with the two of us."

"I'm sure he can. He'll be out by the pond fishing."

"Oh, Tulip will love that! She still misses Frank."

"I know you both do."

"Yes, it's hard being up here without him."

"I'll bet it is. I can't even imagine what it's like."

"I hope you never have to."

"Me too." Then, after a brief pause, she said, "Okay then, see you soon."

"Bye, Ringo, have a good trip."

"Okay, bye."

"We're having company. We're having company," Annie began singing, not even trying to contain the excitement she felt at the prospect of having visitors. And not just *any* visitors, her very best friend in the whole world! Maybe *she* would be able to shed some light on Annie's current dilemma. After all, Ringo had been there during the entire unfolding of all those long-ago, drama-filled events, even as an active player in some instances.

"Come on in, Tulip, I'm fixing lunch. I know you want something too."

Annie was soon back in her chair with another cup of tea. "Now let's see . . . Where was I?"

# 1965

## CHAPTER 31

## "It's Only Make Believe"[31]

"Honey, I'm home" was Frank's standard greeting every evening exactly at six o'clock. It was cute the first few times. Usually, I had some sort of meal planned that we ate around six thirty. I was getting pretty good with meatloaf, hamburgers, and tuna noodle casserole. After dinner, Frank would clean up the kitchen, while I went off to study for the rest of the evening. Our routine didn't vary much for the next two years. I didn't feel like a "married woman." I felt like we were playing house. Sometimes on weekends, we'd invite Beth or Ringo over for dinner. Those times I did feel a little more "married," like I had a secret that all the other girls weren't privy to, a feeling I hadn't anticipated but enjoyed immensely.

"Annie, what's it like actually *living* with a man?" Beth would ask every now and then. "Is it gross sometimes, like when you have to wash his underwear or clean his whiskers out of the sink?"

"No, silly," I'd reply. "Frank usually does the laundry anyway and the bathroom cleaning also. He's not gross."

It was obvious she had other questions she wanted to ask—personal ones—but she never did. And I didn't offer any intimate details about Frank and me. I knew she was wondering, which amused me. One time when she asked if I had any "married woman" tips to share, I explained

---

31. "It's Only Make Believe"; artist: Conway Twitty; released 1959.

that I'd learned to spread out the shower curtain after showering so it wouldn't get mildewed, a lesson I'd learned the hard way.

"Any others?" she persisted.

"Yeah, I found that when cleaning up after dinner, you should put away the meat leftovers first and then the veggies and other stuff. You don't want the meat to stay at room temperature any longer than necessary." This was actually a piece of wisdom that my mother had instilled in me years before, but I didn't tell Beth that. These answers seemed to appease her at the time.

Ringo, though, was another story. Although she refrained from prying into our lives the first few months, she couldn't hold out after that. She began with allusions and suggestive comments like "Now that you're married and having sex all the time . . ." or "I heard about a couple that has sex every night. Can you imagine?" I was intentionally noncommittal in my responses, leaving her to wonder all the more. Finally, one time, she just came right out and actually asked if our honeymoon had been everything I'd hoped it would be. I wasn't ready to confide in her or to give her the satisfaction of hearing the truth about our first sexual encounter, so I lied. "Yes, it was wonderful," I said. Frank was a caring, thoughtful husband; I wouldn't have felt right betraying a confidence about our sex life. Perhaps this pretext of total marital bliss had something to do with my feelings of playing house. It was all just make believe. Which didn't mean that we didn't have a happy marriage. In all other areas, Frank and I were a perfect match. Life with him was comfortable and secure, right from the start, which is just what I had been looking for.

One weekend towards the end of my junior year, Frank had to be out of town for some training, so I took that opportunity to invite Beth, Ringo, and Laney over for a "slumber party." We had also invited Beth's new roommate, Marie, a transfer student from Missouri, to join us, but she already had plans with a fellow Spanish major.

Frank had bought some wine for our little gathering, and I had actually prepared an edible meal. Everyone seemed to enjoy my meatloaf and, of course, the camaraderie. "The four of us together again. It's almost like old times," I said.

"Except for the wine!" Laney added, laughing.

"Yeah, we were never ones to buck the system or break any rules," Ringo added. "Not like that crazy Betty Lou down the hall. She's broken nearly every rule in the book and gotten away with most of it!"

"But her luck may be running out," Beth said. "Annie, did you hear about her latest antics, last weekend?"

"No, I didn't," I replied. "Please enlighten me. What have I been missing out on?"

The three of them all began talking at once, each excited to clue me in on the latest in dorm shenanigans. Beth won out.

"She had her boyfriend, Jason, *in her room!*" she said.

"Oh my god!" I exclaimed. "How did she ever sneak him up there? Dress him like a maintenance man?" We all laughed at the thought of that.

"No one is sure exactly how he got *into* the room," Beth continued. "The big story is how he got *out* of the room. Apparently, someone alerted Betty Lou that Mrs. Bender was coming down the hall, so Jason went out the window!"

"What? From the second floor? How did he do that?" I asked.

"Well, not too successfully," Beth said. "I guess he thought he could make his way over to the balcony off the upstairs lobby and then climb down from there. But it didn't work out. He slipped and fell, landing in the grass below. He still might have gotten away with it if he hadn't broken his ankle."

"Wow! I can't imagine!" I said. "And I'm sure there was no way Betty Lou could deny her connection when they found him there. Everyone knows whose boyfriend he is."

"Also, they questioned a couple of her suite mates about it, and of course, no one wanted to lie for fear of getting kicked out," Ringo said.

"What did they do to her?" I asked.

"They've grounded her. She can't leave the campus for the rest of the semester," Beth said. "Seems rather harsh, but she's lucky she's still here after all she's done."

"She *is* a little ditzy," Laney added. "But it's amazing how much stuff she's gotten away with. Remember that time she was mixing drinks right there in her room?"

I thought back then to the one time I had broken the rules.

"So would you guys have lied for me that time—remember, freshman year, when Ned came to visit and I went off campus for the night without signing out?" I asked.

"Um, yeah, of course, we would have, '*Romeo*,'" Ringo joked.

"It would have been just my luck to have gotten caught the only time I did something illegal," I said. "Thank goodness I didn't, especially if I'd had to depend on *you guys* to vouch for me!" I added.

I should have changed the subject right then, but unfortunately, with a little boost from the alcohol, Ringo kept going.

"You, of all people," Ringo said, looking at me. "Such a goody two-shoes that you'd go to any extreme to keep from breaking a rule, even if it meant getting married!"

"That's not the only reason I got married!" I uttered defensively. But everyone knew she was right, and I didn't want to go there. I decided to change the subject. "Who's ready for some dessert? I tried out this new cake recipe, and it looks amazing . . ."

# 1966

## CHAPTER 32

## "To the Aisle"[32]

My status of being the sole married woman among our friends ended abruptly with our graduation. Most of us had been programmed from early on that marriage was the next logical step after college. My friends' weddings followed almost immediately after our graduation. First was Ringo and Danny's, although theirs was not a large celebration. They both had college loans to repay and had little help from either set of parents financially. Danny's brother, Rick, and I were their "attendants," and along with all the parents, we accompanied them to a scenic spot along the bank of the James River, where they said their vows. Their wedding had a uniquely romantic quality, no doubt because of the setting and because the two were so obviously meant for each other. For their honeymoon, they had planned a camping trip to the Blue Ridge Mountains. They couldn't have been more excited.

Beth and Roger's wedding, on the other hand, was the social event of the summer in Richmond. It was, I knew, the wedding that Frank's parents and grandma had wanted for Frank and me, right there in Grace Episcopal Church, where both Frank and Beth had attended services since childhood. I was Beth's matron of honor, and she had six other bridesmaids. Frank was one of seven groomsmen. It was picture perfect,

---

32. "To the Aisle"; artist: The Five Satins; released 1973.

Beth stunningly beautiful in her long organza gown and Roger equally striking in his white dress Naval uniform.

In truth, it was quite similar to how I had envisioned my own wedding prior to my involvement with Frank, and I had to admit to a tinge of regret that I was not able to live out that dream. Being a part of Beth's extravaganza, however, was the next best thing. Frank and I both thoroughly enjoyed our roles in it and the partying that followed, as well. Their reception was held at the lavish Petersburg Country Club, where Beth's parents were longtime members, and the partying continued long into the night, shifting from the country club to the home of Beth's parents, which was perfectly suited for entertaining.

"This could have been ours, you know," Frank said to me as we were dancing early in the evening, "if I hadn't messed it up by becoming a Martinsburg Townie."

"Our wedding was perfect for us," I said. "It was what was meant to be."

"You mean you don't have any regrets?" he asked. "We could have waited and had one just like this."

"No, no regrets," I replied honestly. "If we had waited till now to get married, our situation would be completely different today."

"Well, yeah, but what exactly do you mean?"

"I just mean we wouldn't be as settled in our marriage as we are and wouldn't be ready to start a family."

"Annie, what are you trying to tell me? Are you ready to start a family?"

"Yes, I think I am," I replied. "And I hope you are too."

"Are you pregnant or something?"

"I was going to tell you before, but well, I'm not sure. I think I am."

"Wow! That's great! Are you excited? Do you feel okay? Do you want to sit down?"

"I'm fine," I said. "I'm just kind of tired in the mornings. I have an appointment to see Dr. Freeman next week to find out. My period's already five weeks late, so it seems pretty certain. I have my hopes up."

"So you're okay with it? I can't believe my baby's growing inside of you! That is so cool! Can we tell people?"

"No, let's wait till we're sure. Besides, this is Beth's day. Let's let her have the limelight."

"Okay, I guess you're right. But jeez! That's so exciting! I'm going to be a daddy! We're going to be a family! I love you, Annie."

"I love you too." We continued dancing, holding each other close.

None of Beth's friends had ever spent much time with Roger—I had only met him once previously—so we made good use of the reception to get to know him better. At first, he appeared a bit aloof but loosened up as the evening progressed, thanks, in no small part, to the alcohol that was flowing freely. He and his fellow Academy graduates even got a bit loud, taking over the microphone from the band at one point and singing their own version of the Navy fight song. Not to be outdone, the other MWC-ites and I then proceeded to perform our favorite, if unofficial, college song, "Standing in the Doorway." Ten of us were up there, dramatically belting out the words as we had done so many times during those four memorable years:

> *Standing in the doorway, telling him goodbye.*
> *He whispered I'll adore you, I'll love you till I die.*
> *Then he turned away and walked right out of my life*
> *that day.*

That's when it hit me; an era of my life had just come to a close. These girls—women—would never be together like that, possibly ever again. We had all vowed, of course, to keep in touch, and we vowed it again that evening when saying our farewells. But I knew it would never be the same. As we went our separate ways, it was anyone's guess as to which would be the friendships that would stand the test of time, which of us would be the faithful communicators.

This realization of finality hit me harder than the others since I was the only one of us to not be leaving Martinsburg. I had few other acquaintances in the town; my life had been at the college. My friends were there. Now they would all be moving to new and exciting places, and I was left behind.

People often cry at weddings; I cried at the reception. With my possible pregnancy and the loss of my friends, I could feel the responsibilities of adulthood breathing down my neck. I felt like I was getting my mother's life, a scary thought indeed. The tears should have been another clue to my condition. The hormones of pregnancy had taken over my body, and my crying continued off and on throughout the reception.

Frank and I attended a total of six weddings that summer. None had the magnitude of Beth's or was as memorable. That was partially because Beth and Roger were no longer around, leaving our little group incomplete. They had left for Roger's new duty station in San Diego the day after their wedding. The Reynolds clan and I were equally devastated by their move.

My pregnancy was confirmed the following week with a due date projected for early February. In September, I began working as a bank teller in a savings and loan in downtown Martinsburg. I secured the job by remaining silent about the pregnancy; had they known, they would have assumed that my intent was temporary employment, that I'd be leaving in a few months for full-time motherhood, an assumption that would have been correct.

# 1967

## CHAPTER 33

## "Baby Love"[33]

My pregnancy was fairly uneventful, which is the best way for a pregnancy to be. Morning sickness never happened. I got sick only two times the whole nine months, and I attributed both episodes to having consumed spoiled food. The only complaint I had was always being sleepy, which made getting out of bed each morning to make it to work on time the most difficult aspect of my condition. That, and having to go through the whole thing without the support of my school pals. Being the first expectant mom in our group, I had no one with whom to compare notes. Instead, I became the "voice of experience" that the rest of the crew relied on for pregnancy advice in the months and years that followed.

The reality of my condition didn't even hit me until the last two months. The hospital offered a course on baby care, which Frank and I eagerly attended. That's when I realized how much I didn't know. I had been concentrating on the birth while ignoring that I was going to be responsible for caring for the product of that birth. I had never even changed a diaper!

My pregnancy bible was a new book called *Thank You, Dr. Lamaze* by Marjorie Karmel, which had been recommended to me by Nurse Renee in my doctor's office. Having recently given birth herself, she

---

33. "Baby Love"; artist: The Supremes; released 1964.

was actually more helpful than my doctor in many areas. I read the book several times and was intrigued by the idea of a non-medicated delivery. I didn't want to miss my baby's birth! Frank was remarkably supportive on this issue and surprised me one evening by sharing his own desires. We had finished dinner, and I was relaxing with my feet up and thumbing through a booklet given out by the hospital.

"I was checking out that booklet last night myself," he commented.

"You were?" I questioned.

"Yeah," he replied. "This is my baby too, and I wanted to get some idea of what we can expect when the big day gets here, the hospital rules and all. What I noticed is that they don't actually say that fathers can't be in the delivery room. They don't even address the issue. I'm thinking that I'd kind of like to be in there with you to see our son or daughter come into the world. How would you feel about that?"

"Well, uh, sure. I think I'd like that. I'll need to ask Dr. Freeman though. I'm sure he'd have to approve. I know that Nurse Renee's husband was there when she delivered, but I thought maybe that was just because she's a nurse. But you're right. If he could be in there, the hospital must not have any rules against it. So I'll ask at my next appointment."

When I inquired, I found that Dr. Freeman was kind of an old country doctor with an "anything goes" attitude. "If that's what you both want, it's fine with me," he said. "But only if you're awake for the birth. He's really there to help and support you, you know. And I haven't lost a daddy yet," he added with a chuckle.

Hearing our discussion, Nurse Renee spoke up and suggested that Frank might like to meet her husband, Bruce. "We don't have any birthing classes to offer for dads *yet*," she said in a reprimanding tone directed at the doctor, but Bruce would be happy to share his experience in the delivery room, and that might make it easier for Frank. In fact, why don't the two of you come to our place Friday evening? We'll cook some hamburgers and talk about placentas and stuff."

"That would be great!" I said, resisting the urge to comment on her mention of hamburgers and placentas in the same breath.

Frank was less than enthusiastic about the idea when I brought it up that evening.

"I can think of many things I'd rather do than sit in the home of perfect strangers and hear the gory details of their baby's birth," he said. "But if you think it's important, I'll go."

Our baby daughter, Grace Barstow Reynolds, was born two months later, with Frank by my side.

Thus began our life as parents . . .

# 1973

## CHAPTER 34

### "Second Honeymoon"[34]

When Grace was born, my life was forever transformed. I never knew such love–such complete and unconditional love–was possible. That perfect little being that Frank and I had created together gave me new purpose. I loved her beyond description. And, coupled with the love, was the nurturing hormone that Mother Nature provides to new mothers during the breastfeeding years. My nurturing hormones were apparently in overdrive. Some days, I just couldn't put her down. Frank would come in at his six o'clock arrive-home time and find me sitting on the couch, gently cradling our sweetly-sleeping little one.

"I'll bet you've been holding her all day, haven't you?" he'd chide, a fact I would always happily admit to. Frank was totally supportive of my mothering techniques, which at that time were not widely accepted. Many "experts" cautioned that too much attention could "spoil" an infant, a theory that was later abandoned, thankfully, in favor of what came to be known as "attachment parenting." At the time, however, I was simply following my instincts.

Frank was, I think, actually proud of my parenting methods, as well as proud of himself for making it possible for me to be a full-time mom. It definitely helped that Grace was such an "easy" baby; Frank felt I must be doing something right.

---

34. "Second Honeymoon"; artist: Johnny Cash; released 1960.

Our vacations during Grace's early years always involved the three of us; Frank and I never went anywhere without her. Because I loved my job as a hands-on parent, I didn't feel the need to "get away." The three of us spent many happy weeks, and weekends, in a rented cabin on the Potomac River at Colonial Beach, sometimes the very same cabin that I had stayed in with my parents during my own growing-up years, the one called "The Golden Owl." Our favorite pastime there was climbing into our rented wooden rowboat and spending the day on the murky river crabbing. Grace learned very early how to patiently wait for those elusive nibbles on the end of her line, and then to carefully pull in the line, inch by inch, so as to not alert the unsuspecting crab that a net was awaiting his arrival at the surface. A good day of crabbing always resulted in a delicious dinner of freshly-caught steamed crabs later in the day.

When Grace was six, Frank suggested that he and I take a trip without her. He had to go to South Carolina on business and invited me to come along. "And then we can spend a night at Hilton Head, a sort of second honeymoon," he said. I was reluctant to leave Grace but finally agreed when my parents volunteered to come stay with her. They had never spent any time alone with her, so I was pleased to see they were willing.

Our departure that Thursday evening was much harder on me than it was on Grace. It turns out she was thrilled to finally have the undivided attention of her Nana and Pop Pop. Knowing she was okay allowed me to relax and enjoy our little vacation. Frank spent Friday working while I slept in and then finished a novel I'd been reading for several weeks. Saturday morning, we headed to Hilton Head.

I was pleasantly surprised to learn that Frank had made reservations at one of Hilton Head's most luxurious hotels, the Leilani, where we spent the afternoon lounging by the pool. He had also made dinner reservations at the famous Brett Charles, a fine restaurant that I had often heard about but never expected to experience in person. I didn't know Frank was even capable of planning such things. I speculated that someone at work had suggested these places to him, but I didn't want to spoil the occasion by asking and risk ruining the magic of the moment.

Luxury hotels and gourmet dining were certainly not the life I was used to, and I wanted to make the most of the occasion. I could tell Frank felt different too, more empowered and in control. We laughed over dinner like we hadn't done in years. And consumed more wine than we had in years as well. Fortunately, we were within walking distance of the Leilani.

As we entered our hotel room, Frank took my hand, looked into my eyes, and announced, "And now, my dear, I am going to make love to you." I felt like I was living someone else's life, or possibly playacting in a movie. Could this be the same man I had been living with for nine years? He then proceeded to, slowly and methodically, remove my clothes, planting kisses on my bare skin as he progressed. When he got down to my panties, I didn't know if I could hold out any longer. I was still standing, just inside the closed door; Frank was kneeling in front of me, kissing my belly. My clothes were scattered everywhere.

He stood up and whispered softly in my ear. "I love you so much, Annie. I know I never tell you enough how much you mean to me. You and Grace are my world. I just want to be the best for you." And then his lips found mine, and we kissed passionately, his tongue exploring the inside of my mouth. He pulled away and led me to the bed. I lay down. He sat next to me and began lightly caressing my lower abdomen with his tongue, causing me to ache with desire. I felt him gently licking the inside of my thighs. Almost there! "Do it," I pleaded. "Do it now!"

Slowly, he moved towards ground zero of my arousal, where the very touch of his soft, moist tongue sent me into orgasmic ecstasy. His continued slow stroking served to prolong my sensations until I thought the orgasm might never end. *When did he learn to do that?* Then he was on top of me, and I could feel his manhood, trying to find its way. I quickly guided him into me, pressing my hips towards him. "Oh Annie, I love you," he mumbled as he stiffened and thrust himself one last time, causing us to climax at the exact same moment, the first time that had ever happened for us.

We fell asleep like that, sort of stuck together and stuck to the sheets as well. I awoke about two o'clock and got up and washed, put on a gown, and got back into bed. Frank didn't budge until morning.

"I had the weirdest dream last night," I said to him as he began stirring.

"What was it?" he asked, one eye open.

"There was a strange man here, and he was making the most glorious love to me," I said.

He opened both eyes and replied, "That was not a strange man. That was your husband. And I hope that makes up, just a little, for our first attempt at a honeymoon."

It did indeed make up for our previous honeymoon, in many ways. Our second daughter, Ashley Leilani Reynolds, was born nine months later.

# 1977

## CHAPTER 35

## "Do You Believe in Magic?"[35]

Frank was a wonderful provider, which, of course, was no surprise. I was confident that would be the case when I married him. He was smart, well-liked, and a hard worker, all of which contributed to his career success. His promotions were steady, along with the corresponding salary increases.

At age thirty-five, Frank was working alongside fellow engineers who were much older and more experienced than he. And from what I could tell, they often looked to him for his ideas and advice. One evening, upon coming home from work, he matter-of-factly announced that he'd been recognized by some science foundation for one of his achievements.

"Remember how I was saying that there should be a way to utilize the by-products of the water treatment process?" he asked as I was cutting up a chicken for dinner.

"Uh, yes, I think so," I responded, only half listening.

"Well, I came up with a possible method for accomplishing that. My boss took my idea to his boss, and they tried implementing it, and it worked! And my boss's boss thinks it's worthy of a bonus—for me!"

---

35. "Do You Believe in Magic?"; artist: The Lovin' Spoonful; released 1965.

"What? No way! That's great!" I responded, turning to him. "I'm so proud of you!" I said, wiping the chicken fat from my hands and giving him a big hug. "We should celebrate!" I added.

"Okay, let's do that," he agreed. "I've been thinking. We've never really taken a family vacation, I mean other than to Colonial Beach."

"The girls *love* Colonial Beach!" I said.

"I know. We all do," Frank said. "But I bet they'd also love a trip to Disney World."

"Disney World? Did you say Disney World?" a small voice questioned from the other room. Ten-year-old Grace had apparently been eavesdropping on our conversation. "Are we going to Disney World?"

"I wanna go to Disney World too," added almost-four-year-old Ashley. "I wanna see Minnie Mouse!"

So it was decided, and we began planning. We set the date for Grace's spring break, nearly two months away, which gave us plenty of time to enjoy the anticipation. The girls were at perfect ages, we decided. Grace had heard many Disney World stories from her friends and couldn't have been more excited. And Ashley, who was in love with Minnie Mouse, talked nonstop about the chance to meet her favorite character. Each morning she'd ask, "How many more days?"

Frank made all the arrangements. We were to fly to Orlando, then rent a car and drive to the Magic Kingdom. We would be spending three nights in Disney's Contemporary Hotel. I could tell he was really proud to be providing this experience to the girls and me, especially rewarding since it was a direct result of his dedication and hard work.

The trip was everything that we had hoped for and more. Beginning with their first airplane ride, the girls were wide-eyed with wonder.

I too was enchanted with all that Disney World had to offer. "This is way more than an amusement park," I said to Frank after we had ridden the monorail from our hotel and were entering the park through the turnstiles. "This is a whole 'other world' experience! What a great idea it was to come here!"

The girls' favorite was, of course, Small World, and, although it took a while, we managed to locate Minnie Mouse and secure a photo of her with Ashley. That photo, alone, was worth the trip as it remained framed on Ashley's dresser for the next ten years.

Our family adventure was not without mishap, however. After getting off the Dumbo ride, Grace complained of a tummy ache. Thinking she was probably just hungry, we headed to the nearest food bar. While waiting in line, we learned that hunger was definitely *not* the problem, as Grace proceeded to throw up, losing what appeared to be everything she had eaten in the past week. Distraught and embarrassed, I wanted to vanish into nothingness. Remarkably, it was Frank who took control of the situation, comforting Grace, apologizing to all, and getting us out of there.

"It's okay, Sweetie. It happens to everyone," he said, handing her his handkerchief. "Let's just go sit over here on this bench until you feel better. Maybe Mom can get us a Coke for you to sip on." At home, sick kids were always *my* department. Who was this person that Frank had transformed into? Perhaps this was indeed the "magic" kingdom!

We spent the remainder of that afternoon back at our hotel, napping. Grace, it turned out, was fine, just a little disoriented from the Dumbo ride. "We have the whole day tomorrow for more excitement," Frank told the girls, "so let's not push ourselves today."

Our second Disney day was, fortunately, less eventful and just as much fun. Avoiding any more "questionable" rides, we enjoyed the merry-go-round, Peter Pan, and Pirates of the Caribbean. Grace and her dad even braved the Haunted House, while Ashley and I shared a cotton candy.

That night, after the girls had fallen asleep, Frank and I were lying in bed, reliving the day's events.

"This was such a memorable time for all of us," I told him. "Thank you for making it happen, not just financially, but for taking care of all the details. You seem to have a real knack for vacation planning," I said, flashing back to our second honeymoon and the luxury accommodations he had surprised me with. "It makes me wonder what other hidden talents you might have that I haven't discovered yet."

"Guess you better stick around to find out," he said.

"I think I will."

# 1987

## CHAPTER 36

## "Dream a Little Dream of Me"[36]

It was a Tuesday afternoon in my forty-fourth year. Daughter Grace was off at college and Ashley in school at the junior high. I returned from the supermarket with the week's shopping and noticed a blinking light on the answering machine. I punched "play" and proceeded to unpack a grocery bag while the tape rewound. *Probably Frank*, I thought. *He's so predictable.* The machine beeped once, and then I heard a voice. It wasn't Frank's. "Hi, Annie. It's Ned Nash. Do you remember me?" My heart jumped. Did I hear that right? "I'm calling about our twenty-fifth reunion. Wondered if you were going. I'll try back later. Hope you're doing okay. Bye."

I couldn't believe my ears! I rewound the tape and listened again. And again. My heart was pounding and my stomach doing cartwheels. It was really Ned! "Oh my god! He's *alive*—and real!" I said out loud. I sat paralyzed while the groceries thawed on the counter. I played the message until I had every word, every pause, every breath committed to memory. "It really is him," I said again, still in disbelief.

He was going to call back. Would he? When? How long would I have to wait? What would I say?

The tasks that had seemed so pressing when I came in the door—starting the casserole for dinner, making a dentist appointment for Ashley, getting the clothes from the washer to the dryer—were all forgotten. The anticipation of his call was all consuming. I sat waiting

---

36. "Dream a Little Dream of Me"; artist: The Mamas & the Papas; released 1968.

for the phone to ring, still not knowing what I'd say. I was wondering how I'd make it through the rest of the day if he didn't call. Fortunately, I didn't have to find out. The phone rang. I grabbed it.

"Hello?"

"Annie?"

"Ned?"

"You remember me?" he asked.

"Of course I do! Are you crazy?"

"Well, I didn't know. It's been a while."

"Ned, I could never forget you. You were my first love. I still have dreams about you." What was I saying?

"You do? What kind of dreams?"

"Never mind. How are you? Where are you?"

"I'm in Colorado. I live here."

"Uh, are you married?"

"Yes. I have a wife and two kids, a boy and a girl. We married late. The kids are little."

"Oh my gosh." I was trying to take it all in.

"Nicole is three. Ned Junior is two."

Ned Junior? *I* was supposed to have Ned Junior! Someone else had *my* baby! I couldn't speak.

"Annie, are you still there?"

"Yes, I just . . . I guess I'm in shock. I didn't even know if you were alive."

"Why wouldn't I be? Had you heard otherwise?"

"No, I hadn't heard *anything*. The last I knew you were in Vietnam. How would I know anything? You stopped writing. I tried to contact your parents, but they had moved. It was awful."

"I'm sorry. But that's all ancient history now. I guess you've been married for a long time. Do you have a family?"

"Yes, two girls. Grace is twenty and Ashley, thirteen."

"I'll bet they're pretty. Do they look like you?"

"Grace does a little, people say."

"I'll bet you're still pretty."

"I'm fat and gray-haired," I lied, not exactly sure why I was doing that.

"That doesn't matter," he said.

Oh my god. What did *that* mean? As his words began to sink in, I could feel something inside me coming alive, something that had been dormant a long time.

"I sure would like to see you," he continued. "How about the reunion? Can you go? I was thinking I might make the trip back there if you were going. It would be just like old times."

"No, it wouldn't. We're both married," I said.

"My wife, Dorothy, she wouldn't be going. She'd stay home with our kids. She thinks I should go though. She just went to hers. Well, it was her fifteenth. I kept the kids. She saw an old boyfriend or two. So how about it? For old times' sake?"

"Wow. I don't know if that's a good idea," I said.

"I think it would be fun. And it's still three months away. You'd have time to get ready, lose all that extra weight, and get the gray out of your hair." I could hear him smiling.

"I don't know. I don't think so." Such a mixture of emotions churning inside me. The same feelings were definitely there, exactly like twenty-five years before. But then there was the anger; why had he dropped me so suddenly? He seemed so glib about it now. And, what *if* the attraction was still there? We couldn't act on it. I'd never do that to Frank. So what would be the point in going?

"What? Annie? What are you thinking?"

"I'm confused," I said. "Would there be any purpose in seeing each other? It's ancient history, like you said. Maybe it would be best to leave it that way."

"Well, let's see. You could tell me all about those dreams you've been having." I sensed he was smiling again. I was too. "Think about it," he continued. "I'll check back with you in a week or so. Take care, Annie. It's good to talk to you."

"You too," I said. "Bye."

"Bye."

"Mom, why is there ice cream melting all over the counter?" Ashley was home.

# CHAPTER 37

## "The Sounds of Silence"[37]

I was quickly thrust back into my afternoon routine. The casserole got prepared, the dentist appointment made, and the clothes dried. I don't remember actually doing any of those things though. My thoughts were elsewhere. Ned was alive! I had talked to him! And he wanted to see me!

"Honey, I'm home." Frank's evening greeting hadn't changed one bit in twenty-three years. "What's for dinner?"

He put down his briefcase, picked up the mail, and plopped down in his favorite chair without ever really looking at me. Sometimes I wondered if he'd notice if I were to dye my hair green. I had even contemplated doing just that, or at least wearing a wig sometime, to test him but never had. I couldn't help wondering if Ned would notice such things after twenty-three years of marriage.

On the other hand, Frank's lack of attentiveness did have its advantages; he was unlikely to pick up on my preoccupation during dinner that evening. My distracted state went totally unnoticed. No need to make any effort to disguise it.

I didn't intend to not be completely honest with Frank about the phone call. I only wanted to wait for the appropriate time. After the dinner dishes were cleared and Ashley had sequestered herself in her room, I approached him.

---

37. "The Sounds of Silence"; artist: Simon & Garfunkel; released 1966.

"I had an interesting call today," I began.

"From whom?" Frank was putting away the clean underwear and socks from the stack I had left on top of his dresser.

"Do you remember Ned, my friend from high school?" I asked, trying too hard to sound casual.

"Ned? Ned? Was that your next-door neighbor?"

"No, the one that I dated. He was in the Army."

"Oh, *that* Ned. Your old boyfriend."

"Yes, that one. He called today."

"What did he want?" The last pair of socks went into their drawer as Frank asked this question. Then he turned around and actually looked at me. I had finally gotten his attention. I suspected that, at that moment, he might even have noticed if my hair had been green.

"He wanted to know if I was going to our high school reunion. You know, the twenty-fifth. It's this year."

"And what did you say?"

"I said I didn't know."

"Well, are you? You haven't said anything about it. When is it? We could drive up to Fort Custis that weekend if you'd like."

I sat down on the bed and didn't answer right away.

"Or did you want to go by yourself?"

"Uh, I don't know. I'm thinking it isn't a good idea."

"What? Going to the reunion or going by yourself?" Frank asked.

"Either one." I paused. "I just . . . well, we had a really strong attraction. And, uh, I wouldn't want to open that can of worms again."

"Okay. Well, whatever you think."

Obviously, he had no idea what I was trying to tell him. And that might have been a good thing. At least I knew I'd made an effort.

I did not attend the reunion.

# 1989

## CHAPTER 38

## "A Teenager in Love"[38]

One afternoon in the middle of her sixteenth year, Ashley asked me if we could go for a driving lesson. She would soon be old enough to have her license, and she seemed excited to get started on the process.

"I can't believe my baby's almost grown!" I responded. "Yes, of course, Honey. Let's do it."

We drove to a nearby church parking lot that was practically empty, and I let her take over. After slowly circling the perimeter of the lot a few times, she apparently felt comfortable enough to carry on a conversation. In retrospect, I wondered if this topic was, in fact, the whole reason for the driving lesson.

"Mom, can I ask you something?" she began.

"Of course, you can," I replied. "What is it?"

"Well, there's this boy in my biology class, and I kind of like him."

"Oh. What's his name?"

"His name is Joe. He's really cute. And funny. And he likes me too."

"How do you know?"

"He told me. He usually comes to my locker before school and walks me to my first class. At lunch, sometimes we sit together. And remember that time you dropped Laura and me off for a football game?

---

38. "A Teenager in Love"; artist: Dion and the Belmonts; released 1959.

Well, he was there with his sister, and we sat together. And we sort of walked around and talked and held hands. And he kissed me."

"Wow! You really are growing up!"

"He's the first boy I've ever really liked. I mean, I *really* like him. I think about him all the time."

Suddenly, I was back in twelfth grade physics class, passing the protractor to Ned and feeling the sparks fly.

"I know how you feel, Sweetie. First loves are so special," I said. I briefly considered telling her about my first love but reminded myself that this conversation was about her, not me. "So what did you want to ask me?"

"Well, here's the thing. He asked me to go with him."

"Go where?" I asked.

"No, not anywhere. Just 'go' with him. That means not go out with anyone else."

"Oh," I said, laughing. "And do you want to 'go' with him?"

"Yes, I think I do. But Laura and the other girls told me I shouldn't. They said I'd be smarter to just 'play the field,' not let him know I like him. But I do like him, and I don't want to lose him, so I don't know what to do."

"Well, here's what I think. First, you should invite him over so your father and I can meet him. Don't worry, we won't be too hard on him, maybe just a few questions. Then, as long as we approve—and I'm sure we will—I think you can't go wrong if you follow your heart."

"Oh thanks, Mom. I think I will invite him over this weekend, like on Saturday. Maybe his sister can drop him off. He could have lunch with us, right? And we could listen to tapes or walk down to the park. Or go to Carl's for a milkshake. I think you'll really like him," she said, smiling. Then she added, "I've had enough driving practice for today. Thanks, Mom. And thanks for understanding."

I thought back again to my days with Ned and the hopes and dreams we'd had. I remembered how I'd planned on marrying him and having a "Ned Junior" someday, and I imagined that Ashley was having similar fantasies with hopes of a "Joe Junior" in her future or maybe "little Joey." I smiled to myself as I envisioned that for her.

I then tried to imagine having a similar "boy" conversation with my mother during my teen years. It was so inconceivable that I couldn't even picture it. Her "sex talk" with me had consisted of a single topic. "There are these things called rubbers," she had said. I was certain that she would not have advised me to follow my heart. How grateful I was that Ashley and I were comfortable talking about such topics.

I knew too that much more needed to be said on the subject of young love, but I felt hopeful that with Ashley having opened the door for discussion, the rest would follow easily at the proper time.

# 1990

## CHAPTER 39

### "Sixteen Candles"[39]

"Hi, Roomie! It's great to see you! I'm glad you all could come!" I said to Ringo as I opened the front door.

"Me too," she replied, rushing in to hug me. "You know we'll use any excuse to visit you guys."

"You look great. Funny how neither one of us ever changes," I said. "We both look just like we did back at MWC."

"Only better," Ringo added. In truth, the two of us *had* taken very good care of ourselves and were both quite proud of our forty-six-year-old bodies.

"We probably *are* in better shape than when we were in college," I agreed.

"Yeah. I don't remember exercise ever being a priority back then," Ringo said, "and once we got to be seniors and had cars, we stopped walking altogether. We drove everywhere, even to the dining hall."

"And now look at us. We both plan our weeks around visits to the gym. And yoga classes."

"Older and wiser, I suppose," she said.

"Let's hope so," I added.

Danny and Erica joined us then, bringing in the luggage.

---

39. "Sixteen Candles"; artist: The Crests; released 1958.

"You know where the guest room is," I said to Danny, pointing to the stairs. "And, Erica, you can put your things in Ashley's room. She even cleaned it for you." Frank and I had expanded and renovated our little Franklin Street house after Ashley was born. We had expanded *up*, adding a new master bedroom and a guest room on the second floor. The house now had four bedrooms and two and a half baths.

We were gathering to celebrate Ashley's sixteenth birthday, which had actually taken place three weeks earlier, but this was the first weekend we'd all been available. Since they had practically grown up together, Ashley's birthday wouldn't have been complete without a celebration that included Ringo's daughter, Erica.

The cool Virginia spring provided an ideal backdrop for our late afternoon cookout. The dogwood trees added to our pink and white theme. We had one of each color in the backyard, and they were in full bloom.

Four of Ashley's school friends joined us for dinner, after which, all the young women retreated to her room to listen to music and engage in boy talk, a pastime far preferable to hanging out with the parents.

Ringo and I tackled the kitchen cleanup, while our men sat in the living room, sharing fish stories.

"Annie and I are talking about getting our own mountain place someday," I heard Frank tell Danny. "A little cabin with a pond right outside the door. It's our retirement dream, but we're hoping we can make it happen sooner. And with Annie now getting paid for her speaking engagements, who knows? Maybe it will be possible."

"That would be a fisherman's paradise," Danny agreed. "I can imagine you guys would be going there every weekend. Hell, *we'd* be going every weekend!" he added, laughing.

I envisioned that too but not till both girls were out of the house. Weekends in the mountains with Ringo and Danny *did* sound like a dream.

Just as we were putting the last glass in the dishwasher, Danny and Frank appeared in the kitchen doorway.

"We know you two will be up half the night talking, so we're gonna hit the hay now," Frank said.

Danny went over to Ringo and wrapped her in his arms. She rested her head on his shoulder, and they stayed that way, not speaking for several moments. Then they kissed. Frank and I stood watching, transfixed by the touching scene. Then he kissed me on the cheek, and we all said good night.

"It was a great dinner, Honey. You did a good job," Frank yelled back to me on his way up the stairs.

"Let's relax with another glass of wine," I said to Ringo, pouring two new glasses for us. "We might as well stay up and talk since it's expected of us."

"It *was* a great party," Ringo said as we settled ourselves in the living room, her in the recliner and me on the couch. "You and Frank always do it right, good food and just the right mix of people. And there's something else too. Everyone always feels comfortable here. That's because of you guys, you know, being such gracious hosts and setting the tone with your own relaxed manner. People appreciate that."

"You two have something special too," I replied. "It's obvious to those around you. You're really soul mates, I think."

"I think so too. We're very lucky."

"Yes, you are lucky. Not many people experience what you have."

"It's true. Danny was my first love, and he'll be my last. We're like two pieces of a puzzle, a perfect fit." She paused and then continued. "Who would have thought *I'd* be the one to find the ideal mate? *You* were the one caught up in the romance drama back in college, *'Romeo.'*"

"That *was* drama," I agreed.

"You and Ned seemed like a perfect fit too back then," she went on, pouring more wine in our glasses as she spoke, just as she was pouring more fuel onto the Ned-Frank controversy once more as only she could do. "I always suspected that *he* was your ideal match."

"You know, I thought so too back then. But obviously, I was wrong."

"I don't think you were wrong, Annie. Just because you're no longer together doesn't mean he's not your one true love. Maybe you'll be together again in the future, if not in this lifetime, in another one."

"Here you go again, trying to stir up trouble, and I don't appreciate it! Frank and I are very happy. We have a good marriage. I'm really lucky to have him. And I will never leave him for Ned!"

"Methinks you doth protest too much," she went on. "I *know* you and Frank are happy, and he's a great guy. But you had a certain glow when you were with Ned, something I haven't seen in you since. It's that extra spark. I'm not putting Frank down. He is one of the good ones, and the two of you work well together. In fact, you have more than most couples. It's just—I don't know how to say this—you *sparkled* with Ned."

I thought about that for a minute. I realized that, once again, she had hit the nail on the head. "I know," I whispered finally. "You're right," I said, letting the feelings come to the surface, the ones I'd suppressed for so long. And with the feelings came the tears. Thoughts of Ned engulfed me, and I suddenly had a vision of what I'd missed out on. I couldn't stop the tears.

For that moment, I allowed myself to go back and experience the memory of our times together, the connectedness of our souls. Sometimes we had been so close that it seemed as if there were only one soul and we were both a part of it. What had happened? It was too sad for words. I sobbed helplessly.

"Oh my god. I'm so sorry," Ringo gasped. "I didn't mean—"

"It's okay," I sputtered, trying to regain control. I was quiet for a minute and then continued slowly. "It feels good to admit it. I've been denying it, even to myself. When you said that just now, it all became clear. I was meant to marry Ned. Only somewhere along the way, it didn't happen. A glitch in the big plan or something. We screwed up. Or maybe the Universe let us down. Ned knows it too. I know he does. And now we're both married to other people."

"I think your heart chose Ned and your head chose Frank," she offered, trying to make sense of it.

I thought of my husband then and realized what I had just said. I quickly tried to retract it. "I mean . . . uh, I *do* love Frank."

"I know, Annie."

"And we *are* happy."

"I know you are."

"And our girls. If I hadn't married Frank, I wouldn't have Grace and Ashley. That's unimaginable!"

"Stop explaining," Ringo said. "I know what you mean."

We sat in silence for a few minutes, sipping on our wine.

"Ringo, you must never tell anyone about this."

"Of course I won't," she said.

"Even Danny."

"Okay, I won't."

"Promise?" I asked.

"Yes, I promise." I knew I could trust her to keep her word. Could I trust myself? That was the question. After all, I had just done the unthinkable. I had admitted that my life with Frank was one big mistake.

# CHAPTER 40

## "Midnight Confessions"[40]

I sobered up quickly after that unplanned and embarrassing admission, and I was, in fact, wide awake when I crawled into bed a little while later. I continued contemplating what I had said and why I had said it. I lay there next to Frank, listening to his heavy breathing, and began looking back at our life together, possibly hoping to find more good than bad in all those years. *So much good,* I told myself. *The security, our girls, our friends, our home. I'm so fortunate,* I thought. *So why do I have to keep convincing myself of that?* And then I knew. It was the sex. Only it wasn't the sex itself; it was his approach to sex, a discovery I had made on our honeymoon. Even though I had known before we were married that Frank was not a passionate man, I didn't realize then what a difference this would make in our marriage.

Our wedding night had begun with a lovely dinner at the Colonial Beach Yacht Club. We returned to our room in the early evening, still laughing and talking about our big day. I remembered the two bottles of champagne that Beth had tucked into my bags as a reminder of that crazy night following Frank's graduation, a night that had resulted in our engagement. "Only I won't be there with you this time," she had said. "You'll have to make your own fun."

---

40. "Midnight Confessions"; artist: The Grass Roots; released 1968.

I dug out one of the bottles and handed it to Frank, suggesting that we open it and make a toast. "To us," we proclaimed in unison after Frank had popped the cork and poured us each a glass. Laughing, we sat down on the bed and continued sipping our drinks. It seemed to me then that it would be an easy transition to a romantic sexual encounter, but Frank began acting uncomfortable.

"Uh, do you want to lie down?" he asked, somewhat nervously.

"I do," I said, "but let me go change first." I went into the bathroom and quickly put on the long white negligee that Beth had helped me pick out. I caught a glimpse of myself in the mirror as I opened the bathroom door. *Is that ME?* I thought. *I look like a goddess! I can't wait for Frank to see me!*

When I came out, Frank was lying on the bed in his jockey underwear. But instead of the adoration I was expecting to see in his face, he was looking at me somewhat sheepishly. "What's the matter?" I asked.

"Uh, I don't know how to tell you this," he said quietly. "I, uh, was just trying to, uh, sort of get in the mood, and well, I couldn't wait."

I looked closely then and saw a wet spot on his underwear. I didn't know how to respond. I felt slighted, disappointed, angry, and many other emotions I couldn't even name. A tear rolled down my face.

"I'm *so* sorry," he said. "It's just I wanted to be good for you, and now I've disappointed you. I've ruined everything!"

I lay down next to him, trying to make the best of it, thinking we could at least have a romantic embrace. "Just hold me," I said finally when he hadn't moved.

He put his arm out for me to lie on, but there was no real touching. I could tell his heart wasn't in it. I guessed he was more concerned with feeling ashamed of what had happened than with sharing any meaningful hugging or caressing. He went to sleep that night without so much as a goodnight kiss.

I, however, lay there wide-eyed after that, trying to process the events of the evening, or, rather, the lack of events. Ringo's admonition kept coming back to me. She had warned early on that Frank's seeming lack of interest in sex was a bad sign. Now it was clear that he'd had little, if any, previous sexual experience, which wouldn't necessarily have been a bad thing. Ned had had no previous experience either, yet he was amazing with me. I vowed right there on my wedding night that, although Ringo had been correct in her assessment of Frank, I would never divulge that to her. It was too embarrassing.

We did finally "complete the act" while on our honeymoon. It was our second, and last, night at Colonial Beach. Frank suggested that he just massage my shoulders and that there be "no expectations," a clue that he was possibly playing some sort of mind game with himself. We had been indulging in Beth's second bottle of champagne and were both feeling relaxed.

I was enjoying the shoulder massage. Then Frank began kissing my neck, and his hands slipped down to my breasts. I could tell he was getting aroused, and I didn't want to say or do anything to spoil it. Then suddenly, he rolled me onto my back and was on top of me, pulling my panties off and pushing frantically. He was barely inside me when his body stiffened, and he moaned slightly. And then it was over for him.

He rolled off me and lay there for a minute, recovering. "Wow, that was great," he said finally. "But what about you?" he asked.

"I'm okay," I said. "I'm not really in the mood any longer." What I really wanted was for him to hold me and tell me I was beautiful and that he loved me, but I couldn't tell him that. Before long, I heard him snoring.

It was several months before we got the sex act down to a somewhat mutually-satisfying system. We had to work at it. I knew sex wasn't supposed to be "work." It certainly hadn't been with Ned. The difference was that, except for a few occasions when he was totally relaxed, Frank seemed to have an emotional barrier; he wasn't willing to just let himself relax and passionately enjoy the moment. He was more concerned with "performing." This also meant I had to wait for him to initiate the lovemaking. If I were to suggest it, or make advances, he felt too "pressured" to perform. Eventually, he suggested that we might get a vibrator for him to use on me, which took the pressure off him. That solution was okay with me, giving me the opportunity to also make use of the vibrator on my own during those long dry spells in our marriage, which became longer and drier as the years passed. I had learned to live without the passion, and the "sparkle" too, apparently.

Still wide awake after having made that incriminating confession to Ringo about Frank, and then having taken the emotional trip back through my years with him, my thoughts again turned to Ned. I tried to imagine how different my life would have been now if I were with him. I couldn't even picture it. Ned and I had been so young and so naive. I knew those facts contributed to the idealized image I had of a hypothetical life with him. I couldn't imagine him lying next to me, snoring. Wondering about "what might have been" seemed as futile as life itself seemed at that moment. *What's our purpose anyway?* I thought. *Who is in charge, deciding what will happen and who will end up with whom? Is it really one big crapshoot? Or is there a plan, a reason for it all? Is there a lesson I'm supposed to be learning here? If so, what is it?* I wasn't feeling any wiser than I'd been twenty-five years earlier.

I eventually drifted off. The next thing I knew, it was morning, and I was having to face Frank. He was standing over me, offering me a cup of coffee. "This might help you get started," he said. "I'm sure you were up pretty late."

I couldn't look him in the eye after what I'd confessed to Ringo. Guilt was oozing out of every pore. I was tempted to apologize to him right then and beg his forgiveness, but of course, I couldn't.

"Thanks," was all I said. I don't think I could have felt any worse or more deceptive if I had actually cheated on him. In some ways, what I'd done was actually worse than cheating, the implications more serious. It didn't help that I saw Frank as one of the most honest and trustworthy people I had ever known. Deception was so foreign to him that he would never suspect it in anyone else. How could I ever make it up to him?

Ringo and I did not speak of my troublesome disclosure at all that morning. She and Danny were in the kitchen, making pancakes, when I got up. They left shortly after breakfast with promises by all to get together again soon.

Using a headache as my excuse, I went back to bed, where I spent the rest of the day.

# 1991

## CHAPTER 41

## "Turn! Turn! Turn! (To Everything There Is a Season)"[41]

*Even sisters sometimes drift apart.* That's what I told myself over the years as I saw the bond between Beth and me growing weaker and weaker. Many factors had come into play, I reasoned, few of which were my doing. First was Roger's life as a Naval officer. He and Beth were continually moving—from San Diego to Washington state, and then to Japan—as he climbed the career ladder. However, even when Roger was assigned to a ship and was gone for months at a time, Beth insisted on remaining in his home port city rather than returning to her hometown as many Navy wives did. She was active in officers' wives' clubs and felt she had responsibilities to be there to support the others. Typical Beth, always taking care of everyone else.

To be fair, the physical distance between us only partially accounted for the growing emotional distance. Even when Roger was stationed in nearby DC, I saw Beth only a few times. Because they never had children, we didn't have parenting concerns in common. Her many club commitments, as well as her involvement in other volunteer activities, gave her a life quite different from mine.

---

41. "Turn! Turn! Turn! (To Everything There Is a Season)"; artist: The Byrds; released 1965.

But there was more. I sensed she had issues with Roger. The times we did spend with them, most often at a holiday gathering with the Reynolds family, Roger seemed to hover, never allowing Beth and me any time alone. Even the often-oblivious Frank noticed it. On one occasion, when Frank deliberately ran interference by involving Roger in a heated discussion of Naval warfare, Beth and I did manage some "girl talk." She'd had a little wine and was unusually talkative, more like her old self. We were laughing about the past and marveling that we were actually grown-ups, living the lives we'd spent so many hours pondering and anticipating during our college days, now with husbands and responsibilities. She and Roger had been married about five years at that time. She suddenly took a more serious tone and, lowering her voice, caught me off guard by asking, "Do you sometimes feel like you're nothing more than a receptacle for Frank?"

"No, not really," I replied, trying to hide my shock at her question, which itself revealed much about the nature of their relationship. I felt bad for her but didn't know what else to say, so I quickly changed the subject.

Additionally, Beth did not attend any of our MWC reunions. They were never "convenient" for her. Most of our news of Beth and Roger came through the grapevine—Beth's mother to Frank's mother to us. The story we were given concerning their childlessness was that after trying unsuccessfully to conceive for several years, Beth had wanted to consider adopting, but Roger "would not hear of it," according to Frank's mom. If this were indeed the case, I could understand why attending our reunions might have been difficult for her. She would have wanted to avoid any questions she was not ready to answer concerning the isolation she must have felt in her marriage.

Being just down the street from the college, I, of course, faithfully attended all the reunions, every five years. What fun it was to bunk in the dorms again, just like old times, and stay up half the night, reliving our college days and catching up on one another's lives. Naturally, every five-year passage brought not just the good news—promotions, babies, and moves—but inevitably, sad news as well—illnesses, divorces, and deaths. Three of our classmates were actually widowed before our ten-year reunion, and two classmates were deceased by then. These events were to be expected, of course, as we got older, and they served to make our times together even more precious. During one of those late-night dorm sessions at our twentieth reunion, Ringo and I mused that you could probably write the same generic news for every class of any given year—a certain number of marriages, births, divorces, and deaths—and then just fill in the appropriate names for each particular class. Even so, news of any tragic event occurring in the life of one of our classmates was always devastating.

A big shock for all of us, which took place just a year before our twenty-fifth reunion, was Beth and Roger's divorce. Given all the clues, it shouldn't have been such a surprise. Frank and I learned of it not from Beth herself but through the usual communication channel. Frank's mom called us with the news.

"Poor Ruth is devastated," she announced. "It turns out Roger had been cheating on Beth for years! Can you imagine?" *Poor Ruth? What about poor Beth?* I thought. I immediately reached out to her, writing a short note expressing my concern and extending an invitation for her to come stay with us anytime. She was living in Mayport, Florida, at that time, Roger's last duty station before their separation.

Less than a week later, an envelope bearing Beth's signature butterfly design showed up in our mailbox. Seeing it, I had a brief flashback to life at MWC and all those butterfly-print letters she so lovingly scripted and sent to Roger. I opened it carefully, not wanting to damage any butterflies.

*Dear Annie,*

*Thank you for your letter and your concern. I appreciate the offer to visit you and Frank. However, I am kind of stuck here in Florida for a while. My doctors are here, and I'll be getting chemo for the next six months. Yes, cancer. I was diagnosed with breast cancer three months ago, right after Roger and I separated. I have already undergone a double mastectomy and have just about recovered from*

> that. I asked my mother not to tell you because I wanted to let you know myself. I am going to be fine, both from the divorce and this. I'm realizing I'm better off without Roger, and I guess my boobs had served their purpose too. Don't worry about me. I'll keep you informed.
>
> Love, Beth

I was stunned! *Poor Beth! Going through all that by herself!* I felt terrible for her and somewhat guilty for not having been a better friend. That evening, we called Frank's mom.

"Did you know Beth had cancer?" Frank asked her.

"Yes, Dear. Ruth told me. But she made me promise not to tell. Beth didn't want people worrying over her. She's had the surgery, and now she's on the mend."

*Dear, sweet Beth, not wanting anyone to worry about her. Still putting others before herself,* I thought.

"Annie's thinking about going to stay with her for a bit while she's having chemo," Frank said to his mom.

"Oh, she doesn't have to do that. Ruth is going. She will be there with her. You needn't be concerned."

Despite my intent at the time to be more proactive in supporting Beth, I neglected to follow through. My family and other activities took precedence, and Beth made it easy to back out of my offers to visit by continually insisting "I'm doing fine" or "Mom's here with me now, so there's no need."

In truth, I *was* quite busy. I had just started taking a college course in food and nutrition, which required my traveling to DC every Saturday for the weekly class at American University. My interest in the connection between good nutrition and good health had begun during my breastfeeding years when I had learned through La Leche League that breastmilk was the ideal food for babies. It was, I found out, the ultimate in natural, unprocessed, and organic food and the one Mother Nature had intended for young humans, bringing them optimum health. I wanted to continue providing the healthiest meals for my family past the baby years and had done much reading to find out what Mother Nature had intended for older humans. I had already given a few talks locally on childhood nutrition based on my La Leche League training and my own research, but I recognized the need to establish some real credentials if I were going to continue lecturing and be taken seriously. Spending any time away from home right then would have sidetracked my plan when it was just getting started.

As it turned out, Beth was not doing fine. We found out later that the cancer had spread to her lungs and then her brain. I never even had a chance to say goodbye. Her mother explained, after the fact, that Beth didn't want her friends to see her "like that." She died in 1991. She was only forty-seven. At her funeral, I mourned the loss of the Beth I used to know, my sweet and caring college roommate who was always looking out for my best interest, the one who helped plan my wedding and had hopes of the two of us raising our children together, a dream that disappeared after her marriage to Roger. I mourned for the Beth who had ceased to exist many years before. The unbearable sadness of lost dreams and lost lives hit me hard that afternoon. I wept inconsolably.

# 1994

## CHAPTER 42

### "Searchin'"[42]

Frank and I didn't normally talk while we were in the car; he was usually driving, and I was most likely reading. Plus, we found that, when we were spending the whole day together, there just wasn't that much to talk about. Of course, the weather was always a good topic, and gas prices, but when you're with someone all day, you can't exactly ask them where they went for lunch or tell them whom you ran into that afternoon.

The two-hour drive to the mountains on that Tuesday in the fall of 1994 was, like most others, without conversation. Our mission was one we'd been planning for years. We were in search of a reasonably-priced, cozy little mountain cabin. It was to be our weekend getaway, the fulfillment of a dream for the two of us. My having turned fifty earlier in the year was a stark reminder that we weren't getting any younger, motivating us to begin pursuing this dream.

We had an appointment with a realtor at two o'clock in a little town on the outskirts of Waynesboro, located on the side of a mountain. We arrived an hour early.

"We have plenty of time," Frank said. "Do you want to get some lunch? I see a Burger Barn drive-in up ahead."

---

42. "Searchin'"; artist: The Coasters; released 1957.

"Let's investigate a little further and see what else we can find," I replied.

"Okay," Frank said. He was usually respectful of my wishes when it came to eating, and he always tried to accommodate them. He knew I'd prefer something a little healthier than fast-food offerings. We kept driving in search of something less processed and more veggie-like.

"Oh look!" I exclaimed as we turned the corner. "That place on the right looks interesting," I continued, noticing that Frank was already pulling into a parking spot in front of "The Greens Deli."

"I think I like this town," I said as I was enjoying my fresh organic salad.

"I do too," Frank agreed, biting into his grilled chicken sandwich. "I hope this is a sign," he added.

We arrived at Pine Mountain Realty exactly at two o'clock and found our realtor, Paula, waiting for us. "I have three places to show you," she said. "I think they are just what you're looking for."

As we pulled up to the first option, I knew it was not the one for us. "Keep an open mind," Paula advised as if she knew my thoughts. "A coat of paint, a few repairs, and a little landscaping and this could be your dream house." I didn't think so.

"Even with those costs," she added, "it's still within your budget."

Frank's one requirement for our possible purchase was having access to a pond suitable for fishing. Option 1 did have a pond nearby, which Paula assured us was well stocked with fish.

"What do you think, Hon?" Frank asked me. I knew that meant he would have been okay with that one.

"Let's see the others first," I suggested. Frank knew that meant I *wasn't* okay with it.

Option 2 was somewhat better, but I wasn't pleased with the layout. There had obviously been many additions, each one seeming like an afterthought. It was haphazard and rambling. Fortunately for me, the pond was quite a distance from the house.

"Uh, that would be a long trek carrying all my fishing gear," Frank said. "And especially long if I'm hauling back a ton of fish."

Paula had saved the best for last. I loved option 3 the moment we drove up. Nestled among a small grove of pines, it invited us to investigate further. What we found was a cozy cabin needing no immediate repairs or upgrades, just the right size for the two of us, with a spare room for guests. And the pond was at the end of a short path.

"So scenic," I said.

"And the price is right," Frank added.

We made an offer that very afternoon, and we were soon the proud owners of a weekend mountain retreat, where we would be spending many happy hours.

# 2009

## CHAPTER 43

### "Manic Monday"[43]

That Monday morning in late June 2009 began like most others had in the five years since Frank's retirement. We got up about eight o'clock, had coffee, watched a little of the *Today* show, checked out the morning newspaper, then had some cereal. If I'd been paying closer attention, I might have realized things weren't right. Frank didn't eat much, and he kept complaining of being tired. The truth was, I was tired too. We'd spent a week up at the cabin, doing a massive cleaning and upkeep of the place, including clearing some brush near the house. Frank had worked harder than usual and deserved to be tired. We'd come home late Sunday night in order for me to keep my Monday morning speaking engagement. I didn't give much thought to his complaints. We were both feeling the effects of our week of physical labor.

Around nine thirty, he announced that he was going to lie down for a bit, and he headed upstairs to the bedroom. Although a morning nap was unusual for him, I still attributed it to too much yard work. I was due to give my nutrition talk to the Martinsburg Women's Club at eleven o'clock, so just before ten o'clock, I went up to the bedroom to get dressed for my presentation. Opening the door, I was shocked to find Frank lying on the bed, clutching his chest and gasping for breath.

"Oh my god! What happened?" I shouted.

---
43. "Manic Monday"; artist: The Bangles; released 1986.

He didn't answer but kept gasping for air. I grabbed the phone and dialed 911.

"Come quick! Send someone now!" I screamed at the phone. "I think my husband's having a heart attack!"

What happened then was a blur of panic and chaos—Tulip barking, men rushing in, loading Frank onto a stretcher and carrying him out. I followed blindly, forgetting to lock the door. I was shaking all over.

Martinsburg Hospital was just a short drive. A nurse met me at the door and led me to a seat.

"Dr. Frederick is with your husband," she said, "getting him stabilized. He'll be out to talk to you soon."

I couldn't stay seated. I paced, still shaking, until an olive-skinned fortyish man in white scrubs appeared.

"Mrs. Reynolds?" he asked in a quiet voice.

I nodded. "How is my husband?"

"I'm afraid he's had a serious heart attack. He is stable now, but the next twenty-four hours are critical. We're monitoring him closely, and we'll do everything we can. He's got the best of care."

"Is he in pain?" I asked.

"No, he's resting comfortably."

"When can I see him?"

"You can see him now. Follow me."

Frank was hooked up to tubes and wires and appeared to be sleeping but awoke immediately when Dr. Frederick said, "Your wife is here."

I took his hand, and a tear rolled down my cheek.

"Don't cry," Frank whispered. "I'll be fine. I think I got here just in time."

"Don't talk," I said. "Save your energy. I'll stay with you. The doctor said the next twenty-four hours are crucial."

"What?" Frank whispered. "I'm *not* going to die," he asserted.

"Of course you're not," I agreed.

Then he dozed off. I knew he must be drugged. I continued holding his hand, but it went limp. He slept for several hours, and I stayed by his side, worrying and praying. When he woke up, he seemed stronger.

"Annie," he said, startling me, "it's been a great life. You've been everything to me."

"Frank, I love you too."

"No, I mean I want to thank you for marrying me and being a loving wife."

"Why are you saying this?"

"In case I don't make it. I need for you to know that."

"I *do* know it," I said.

"We've had forty-five wonderful years," he continued. "It's more than I ever deserved." He paused and took a breath. "And I'm so grateful. I know you would have rather been with someone else . . ."

I couldn't believe my ears. "Frank, what are you saying? Are you delirious?"

"No, I'm absolutely clear headed. Remember that night when Ashley was a teenager and Ringo and Danny came over for the night?"

Of course, I remembered it. I'd thought about it so many times. But hearing Frank say those words sent a chill down my spine.

"Uh, yes, I think I remember," I stuttered.

"Well, I *heard* you. I heard what you told Ringo. I came back downstairs to get some water, and I could hear you all talking from the kitchen. You said our marriage was a mistake, that you should have married someone else."

"No, Frank, no! I didn't mean that! I'd been drinking. I love *you*. Please don't—"

"It's okay, Annie. I've come to terms with it. I should have let you go then, but I just couldn't." He was crying.

I got up and took his face in my hands. "Don't say that, Frank. I love you. I have no regrets. It's been a wonderful forty-five years—our life, our girls, our grandchildren. It's been perfect. You just need to get better so we can have more years together."

The nurse came in and interrupted us. "We need to check some things, Mrs. Reynolds. Why don't you go home and get some rest? You can come back in the morning. He'll be in good hands, and we'll let you know if there are any changes."

How could I leave then after that revelation? But I did. I leaned over and kissed Frank on the forehead.

"I love you very much," I whispered. I wished we could have embraced, but with all the tubes, it wasn't possible. I turned and left the room and headed home to feed Tulip. The day had been a living nightmare.

Of course, I couldn't sleep. I kept the TV on for company, watching it mindlessly. At twenty minutes past three, the phone rang.

"I'm so sorry, Mrs. Reynolds," the voice said. "Your husband had another heart attack. There was nothing we could do."

# 2011

# CHAPTER 44

## In the Cabin
## "Girl Talk"[44]

On Saturday, Annie awakened with the sun, excited about her anticipated houseguests who were due to arrive around noon.

"We've got to get this place ready for company," she announced to her oblivious pup. "This will be the first time we've had visitors, just the two of us, that is." Tulip lifted her head, looked at Annie quizzically for a moment, then, realizing that no treats were involved, slowly stretched her legs out and lay her head back down to resume her snooze.

Even though it had been two years since Frank's passing, Annie had only been to the cabin three times, and those had been for maintenance purposes and never by herself. Grace and Ashley had made sure of that. Her first visit without Frank had been the hardest. A neighbor had notified her after a storm that a fallen tree was blocking her driveway. Grace had insisted on accompanying her mom on that first trip, where together, they met with the "tree man" whom the neighbor had recommended, and they assessed the damage. Fortunately, the house itself was untouched, and the hapless tree was soon cut up and removed. They stayed at the cabin only one night, long enough to make sure everything was in working order and to engage a local realtor to manage the property in the future.

---
44. "Girl Talk"; artist: TLC; released 2002.

Afterwards, Annie was thankful for the tree incident. Not only had it required her to get past that first dreaded cabin visit, but it had also enabled her to prove to herself that she was indeed capable of handling such issues on her own, an empowering discovery, one of many she was to experience during those first two years of widowhood.

Now Annie was hopeful that this imminent visit from her closest friend might provide the opportunity for some "girl talk" for the two of them. Although Annie liked Danny well enough, she wasn't comfortable sharing her personal stories with him. She realized that she and Ringo had not had any meaningful "alone time" since Frank's passing. They'd had weekend get-togethers and even a New Year's celebration but never any time for just the two of them, their "therapy" time as they liked to call it.

Annie knew she was overdue for this much-needed therapy. She'd been processing Frank's deathbed confession on her own far too long, and she was ready for another perspective. Along with the grief she experienced following his unexpected and untimely departure, she'd also been filled with guilt. *How could I have been so careless in my comments that night? The pain poor Frank must have silently endured all that time, nine years!* She even convinced herself that carrying around that hurt had probably been a contributing factor to his heart attack, which meant she was, in some ways, responsible for his death.

*I should have found a way to confide in Ringo back then, right after Frank's passing,* she thought. *Those were the darkest of days.* At the time, her family and friends had, of course, attributed her distraught mental state solely to the loss of her spouse, not knowing she was also blaming herself for it.

After about six months, however, she began acquiring a new perspective, one built around anger. *He should have told me what he'd overheard,* she reflected. *How deceitful of him, "Mr. Integrity," to not let me know. We could have talked about it and possibly cleared the air and gotten past it,* she told herself.

*And then to confess on his deathbed that he'd had that knowledge all those years! That was just plain cruel! How mean and unloving!* With those thoughts dominating her psyche, she spent the next several months being furious at him.

Now she was just confused, and she knew she needed to get a handle on her feelings in order to move on with her life. *Move on or move backwards?* she asked herself, pondering what her future might look like. *I really need to hear Ringo's thoughts on all this,* she concluded.

Fortunately, the opportunity presented itself that very afternoon. Shortly after their arrival, Danny excused himself to go check out the fishing gear and then head towards the pond with the anticipation of providing a fresh fish dinner. Tulip was happy to accompany him down the path to the water. Annie and Ringo were alone in the cabin.

"I know it's a bit early for happy hour," Annie said to Ringo, "but I'm going to have a little wine. Would you like some?" she asked, retrieving two glasses from the shelf.

"Sure, why not?" Ringo responded. "It's always a good time to celebrate when we're together."

"Yeah, eat, drink, and be merry," Annie said. "Who knows what tomorrow may bring?"

"That's for sure," Ringo agreed.

They raised their glasses together and each took a sip.

"We'll start with wine and finish up with rocky road ice cream," Annie quipped, realizing that she was intentionally delaying the more serious conversation that she so desperately needed to have. She was relieved when Ringo took the first step for her.

"How ARE you doing, Annie?" Ringo asked, setting her wine down and leaning forward in her seat. "We haven't had a good therapy session in quite a while, so now's our chance to catch up. I can only imagine how hard this whole thing has been on you. You seem to be getting on with your life just fine, but I'm sure there's more to it than meets the eye. You know you can tell me anything—your deepest, darkest secrets—and they are safe with me. Even Danny can't pry them out of me, not that he wants to," she added with a chuckle. "So how are you doing, emotionally?"

"You might be sorry you asked," Annie responded after a slight pause. "But since you did, here goes. It's a long story, so I'll start at the beginning. Remember that time you guys came to visit when we were celebrating Ashley's sixteenth birthday? You and I stayed up late, talking..."

Annie carefully related every detail of Frank's deathbed confession. Every word of that conversation had been seared into her brain, and now she relived it out loud for Ringo just as she had relived it so many hundreds of times in her mind.

"Those were his last words to me," she said finally. "Our very last conversation and he's telling me of the hurt I'd caused him. Then the nurse came in, and I had to leave." She paused and took a breath. "I never saw him again." She was crying now.

"Oh, Annie, I'm so sorry! I had no idea! What a horror story!" Ringo said, moving closer to embrace her dear friend. She continued to hold Annie in her arms, allowing her the freedom to cry it out.

The tears subsided finally, and Annie pulled away. "I think I needed that," she said softly.

"I can't believe you've been carrying that weight around for two years," Ringo said. "I wish you'd shared that with me sooner."

They sat quietly for a few minutes, Annie composing herself. She got up and went to wash her face, then returned to her seat.

"I can imagine the guilt you felt about this," Ringo offered finally. "What a horrible way to have things end."

"Yes, I did feel very guilty initially, almost like I had actually caused his death. It was unbearable."

"But then you saw the light, right?"

"What?" Annie responded.

"You realized it wasn't your fault at all?"

"Well, yes, sort of," Annie replied. "But what exactly do you mean?"

"He was a jerk!" Ringo said. "He heard us that night, and he pretended he didn't! He kept that from you all those years! How deceptive was that! And then he blurts it all out as he is dying? He should have just taken it to his grave with him! What was the point of telling you then except to cause you pain?"

"I sort of came to that conclusion too eventually," Annie said. "It was mean and hurtful. But on the other hand, maybe he didn't know he was dying. Maybe he just saw it as a chance to be honest, and we could have had a fresh start from there or something."

"You can speculate till the end of time. He did what he did, and it was hurtful. I'm just sorry you went through all that alone. You should've called me."

"I know. I almost did. But at first, I felt so guilty I didn't want anyone to know. And then when the anger set in, I wasn't sure what to think, what was even real. Finally, I knew I needed to hear your thoughts."

"Well, now you've heard them," Ringo said. "And here's more: I think he was a selfish, inconsiderate bastard to do that to you. I also think," she continued after a brief pause, "that, for your own good, you've got to put it behind you. You can't let that one thoughtless disclosure cloud the memories of your many wonderful years together, raising a family—your two beautiful daughters and those sweet grandchildren—your weekends at this idyllic little piece of heaven that you created together and that you both loved so much. Those are the aspects of your life with Frank that you need to focus on for your own peace of mind, and in order to move on."

They sat in silence for a bit. Then Annie spoke. "There's more," she stated quietly, almost in a whisper. "It's about the 'moving on' part."

"ANNIE, DO YOU HAVE A FILET KNIFE?" Danny's voice boomed from the open doorway, startling the women and interrupting their conversation. They both jumped up and headed to the door, curious as to exactly what Danny intended to filet.

"Hold that thought," Ringo said to Annie. "We'll continue this soon right where we left off."

# CHAPTER 45

## "Reach Out I'll Be There"[45]

Later that evening, after they had feasted on the freshest of bass, expertly fileted by Danny, then coated in cornmeal and delicately fried in grapeseed oil, complemented by Ringo's creamy garlic mashed potatoes and a salad of fresh veggies prepared by Annie, along with a bottle of pinot grigio, and all had participated in a quick clean up, Danny announced that he was going to bed.

"I'll be getting up at the crack of dawn," he said. "The best fishing is at sunrise," he added. "Maybe we can have fish and grits for breakfast!" He gave Ringo a warm embrace and a tender kiss and then headed down the hall to the guest room.

Annie and Ringo were soon settled back into their seats in the cabin's cozy living room, Ringo on the couch and Annie in an overstuffed armchair. Frank's recliner continued to sit empty. *I hope Frank's ghost is not occupying that chair right now,* Annie mused.

"Okay, go!" Ringo commanded. "You were just about to tell me how you're 'moving on.' I'm all ears."

Annie cleared her throat and took a deep breath. "Do you remember Ned?" she asked meekly.

"Of course I do! Are you kidding?" Ringo replied. "What? Have you seen him? Is he back in the picture?"

---

45. Reach Out I'll Be There; artist: the Four Tops; released 1966.

"No, not exactly," Annie said. "But sort of. Maybe he could be. I just don't know..."

"Tell me what's going on," Ringo said. "Start at the beginning."

"Okay, it was just over three months ago. Out of the blue, I got an email from him. He said he was sorry to hear I'd lost my husband. That was about it. I wrote back and thanked him. At first, I wondered how he even knew, but I realized he must be getting the postings from this girl—I mean woman—Susan from our high school class who sends emails out with news of our classmates every six months or so. She had written a blurb about Frank's passing last year. He could also have gotten my email address from her. She has everyone's. The last time he and I had communicated, I didn't even have email!"

"So how did you feel, hearing from him?"

"Surprised. Shocked. Stunned," Annie said. "That was the last thing I was expecting."

"Yeah, but did your heart do a little dance when you saw his name on your email?"

"Honestly, yes, it did. But I didn't know what to think. Did it mean something, or was he just being courteous, offering his condolences?" She was lost in thought for a moment, actually pondering the possible implications.

"Is he still married?" Ringo asked, causing Annie's abrupt return to the present.

"I guess so. I haven't heard otherwise. He didn't mention her, Dorothy, I think."

"Have you heard anymore from him?"

"Yes. About a week later, I got another email. He said he wanted me to know that he was there for me if I needed anything."

"Wow. Sounds suggestive. What did you say to that?"

"I just said 'thanks.' I kept reminding myself of the conversation we'd had so many years ago when he called about our twenty-fifth high school reunion. I told him then that we shouldn't open that can of worms, so to speak. We just couldn't go there again. He has respected that all these years. We both have. But now... maybe he's getting senile or something."

"Anymore correspondence after that?"

"Yes, two more times. In the first, about a month ago, he asked how I was doing and offered again to 'be there' for me if I needed anything."

"What did you say to that?"

"Nothing. I didn't reply. I figured I had said it all before, that we shouldn't go there. I don't think the two of us can just 'be friends.' Things between us were way too hot for that, too much animal magnetism, as they say. It's easier—and smarter—to just keep our distance. I guess I'm afraid of being hurt again. You know, 'once burned, twice shy,' or whatever that old saying is. I loved him so much back then, and he broke my heart. I'm too old to go through that again!"

"Maybe it would be different now," Ringo offered. "You need to find out if he's still married. Seems like if he's not—"

"I know," Annie interrupted. "I've been over and over each scenario in my head. In his last email about a week ago, he suggested that we get together and talk, 'for old times' sake.' I didn't respond to that one either."

"Annie, you're in denial!"

"No, I'm not."

"See?" They both chuckled.

"The thing is," Annie said, "I do appreciate your input, but what would be the point, especially if he's still married?"

"Maybe he isn't," Ringo said. "Maybe he's divorced. Or separated. Or widowed. You need to find out."

"Yeah, I guess," Annie agreed. Then she added, "I'll do that."

# 2011

## CHAPTER 46

## "The Answer Is Blowing in the Wind"[46]

I type "Dear Ned." *No, that's not good. I don't want to imply any intimacies.* I delete "Dear Ned." I type "Hey" in its place, a more noncommittal greeting. *Okay, now what?* I continue typing. "I got your last two messages, and I need to ask you a couple of questions before I decide if we should see each other. The first one is pretty straightforward. Are you still married? Thanks, Annie." *Why am I thanking him?* I delete "Thanks." *That's it. Short and to the point.* I press "send."

I relax in my chair and breathe a sigh of relief. *That wasn't so hard,* I decide. I think back to my week with Ringo. *What a dear she was, indulging me like that, providing support, and helping me see what I need to do. If he IS still married, things will end right here. If he's not married, well, then I'll have a decision to make. Do I risk getting hurt again? But would there be any harm in just seeing him? Maybe I could get an explanation of why he dropped me like that, a lifetime ago. What could he say that would negate the pain I went through?* I sit back and wonder how long I'll have to wait for his response.

*I miss Ringo. I should have written to Ned while she was still here. She could have helped me pass the time while waiting for him to answer.*

---

46. "The Answer Is Blowing in the Wind"; artist: Peter, Paul and Mary; released 1962.

"You've got mail," my computer announces matter-of-factly. My heart is jumping as I see that it's from Ned. I scramble to read his response, almost deleting it in the process.

> *"Dear Annie, no, I am not married. Dorothy and I separated almost a year ago, and our divorce is now final. I can provide all the gory details if you let me come see you. The visit wouldn't have to mean anything, unless, of course, you want it to. :) At the very least, we can be old friends just catching up with each other. Let me know. I could be there tomorrow. Your old pal, Ned"*

*Hmmm, so we're "pals" now? Interesting. As if we've been friends all these years? Tomorrow? He could be here tomorrow!* My heart is pounding at that thought. *He doesn't even know where I am. Or does he? Should I tell him and let him come here, this cabin that was Frank's and my sacred place? What if he's become a serial killer and murdered Dorothy? He could do the same to me out here in the woods!* I chuckle at that thought. *That's so far from the realm of possibility for the Ned I used to know. The real question is whether this is our chance to finally be together after all this time. But first, another question.*

I press "reply" on his email, and I start typing. "Ned." *That's a good start,* I muse. *Let's just get right to it,* I tell myself. I continue writing.

"I have a couple more questions, and they are not quite as clear cut. Before I agree to see you, I need to know why you ended it with me all those years ago. I know that's ancient history, but you made the decision to vanish right out of my life with no real explanation. Can you give me an explanation now and help me understand why you did that?" I press "send."

*What can he possibly say?* I wonder. *That he was too young? That he was caught up in the war? That he met someone else? I wonder what the TRUTH is.*

*I can't just sit and wait for his reply. It could take a while.* I get up and let Tulip out. I make a cup of tea. I check the email again and find nothing. I consider taking a shower but decide against it. I pace around the room.

"You've got mail," my computer announces again in its distinct tone, devoid of emotion. I rush back to the screen.

> *"Annie, I did it for you. I told you that at the time. It was the hardest thing I've ever had to do."*

*He did it for me?* "I still don't get it," I type. "You did it for *me*? That doesn't make sense. You broke my heart."

His reply comes immediately.

> *"It broke my heart too. Please let me come see you, and I will explain everything."*

*Maybe he IS senile and doesn't remember clearly. There's no reasonable explanation for what he did.* I can feel my anger rising, and I take a deep breath. *He needs to accept responsibility.* Yet something is telling me I should see him and give him the opportunity to explain, if only to give me closure. *Who am I kidding? I KNOW I will see him! I can't believe this is happening!*

"All right," I type. "You can come here tomorrow afternoon, around three o'clock." *What am I doing?* I give him the address and directions to the cabin. "See you then," I write, just like "seeing" him is a routine occurrence.

*Oh my god! How am I going to pass the time till tomorrow at three?* I text Ringo.

> *"OMG. He's NOT married, and he's coming here tomorrow!"*

I grab the duster and start dusting everything in the house. I pass a mirror in the hallway and see myself in it. *What can I do with my hair? Did I even bring any makeup? What shall I wear?* I go to my closet and flip through the "mountain clothes" hanging in there, mostly jeans and flannel shirts. I check the drawers in my dresser and pull out a pink tank top. I go back to the closet and find a pink plaid flannel shirt. *This might work. Which jeans though?* I find three pairs and try them all on. I decide on the second pair. They're a bit stretchy and tight-fitting, accentuating what curves I have left. I lay the outfit on a chair. I decide to wash the bed sheets. I rip them off the bed and head to the washer. *What am I thinking? Am I crazy?*

I get out the vacuum and start vacuuming. Tulip is looking at me like I've lost my mind. She may be right.

I scrub the bathroom floor and the sink, toilet, and tub. I look for a candle in the cupboard under the sink. I find a partially-burned green one leftover from a Christmas that we spent here at the cabin. I dust it off and find a small plate for it in the kitchen. *Should I leave it on the bathroom counter or put it in the living room?* I can't decide. I set it on the dresser in the bedroom. *What am I doing?*

I decide to look for some fresh flowers before it gets dark. "Come on, Tulip. We're going outside," I call. She jumps up from her nap and happily joins me. I find wild flowers in both blue and yellow. *These will make a cute bouquet.* I take them inside and arrange them in a glass of water.

# CHAPTER 47

# "The Long and Winding Road"[47]

*It's almost time—quarter of three! I can't stand it much longer. I haven't slept. I haven't eaten. This isn't healthy.*

I go to the front door and look out. I see a car headed up the driveway! It's a small SUV, one of those five-seater models, in dark gray. *Is that Ned? I didn't ask him what he would be driving. Oh crap! It's turning around. Someone must be lost. This is too much to handle!* I go into the bathroom and check myself in the mirror. *Not too bad for sixty-seven,* I decide. I run a brush through my now-graying hair. *At least I HAVE hair. I wonder if he is balding . . .*

I hear a light knocking on the front door. Tulip is barking. "No, Tulip, it's okay," I say, rushing to the door and trying to pretend I'm not rushing as I go to open it. My hand is so sweaty it slips off the doorknob. I finally get the door open, and there he stands. I take in the scene—the same Ned, a little older, a little thicker, his sandy hair a little lighter and still tickling his forehead. And he is still adorable.

He speaks first. "Hi, Annie. We've got to stop meeting this way." The twinkle in his eyes is strangely familiar. He leans in and gives me a quick hug.

"Hi yourself," I say unimaginatively, flashing back to that first ever encounter in physics class. *Have I learned nothing in all these years?*

---

47. "The Long and Winding Road"; artist: The Beatles; released 1970.

"Come in," I say, attempting to act composed. "Would you like a glass of drink?" *Oh shit! What is wrong with me?*

Ned is grinning. "Relax, Annie," he says. "We're just two old friends who haven't seen each other in a long time."

"I know, a very long time," I say, resisting the urge to add "Thanks to you who broke my heart all those years ago." My stomach is doing flips.

"Should we sit down?" he asks, pointing to the living room. *Who is the host here?*

"Yes, please," I stammer. We sit, me on the couch, him in Frank's recliner. *This is weird . . . seeing him in that chair.* I decide to resort to small talk.

"So what have you been doing all these years?" I ask.

"Oh, Annie, do you really want to know, or are you just making small talk?" he asks with a grin. *How does he know?*

"I *do* want to know," I say honestly. "Have you been living in Colorado all this time?"

"Yes, I moved there when I got out of the Army. Do you remember I worked there one summer?"

"Of course, I remember."

"Well, that's when I decided I'd like to settle there someday. So I applied to the University of Colorado and went there, thanks to Uncle Sam, you know, the G.I. Bill. I worked part time too, on a ranch. After college, I got a job teaching high school. Physics. I did that for thirty years. Just retired last year."

"Wow, my friend Ringo was a teacher too, elementary school," I say.

"Didn't I meet her that night I came to visit you at college?" he asks.

"Oh yes, she was the one who arranged our little getaway. Dear Ringo. She's still my best friend."

"That was quite a night," he says. "I've thought about it a million times—our last night together . . ."

"I know," I say. "I have too."

"You're just as beautiful now as you were then," he says. He's smiling that shy smile and looking right at me. I don't know what to say. I take a deep breath.

"Before you say anything else," I say, "I have questions. Can you please tell me what happened all those years ago? Why you stopped writing?"

"It was for you," he says. *I don't want to hear that again.*

"Exactly *how* was it for me?" I ask.

"Because I knew I was making you unhappy," he says. "I just couldn't continue causing you so much misery."

"I don't understand why you thought that," I say. "I missed you, sure, but I missed you more when you stopped writing," I tell him.

"Obviously, you got over me though. You found someone else and got married pretty quickly," he says.

"Only because I couldn't have you," I try to explain. "I still don't know why you thought you were doing me some sort of favor when you broke it off. It doesn't make sense."

"It's what everyone knew," he says. "You were so miserable you wanted to die."

"Who told you that? What? Did my mother write you and tell you that?" I ask, feeling my blood starting to boil at that thought. "Did she?" I demand again. "Is that what happened—my mother meddling in my life? *She's* the one who broke us up? How could she have done that to me?"

"No," he replies softly. "Not your mother."

"Who then? Who told you that?" I'm almost yelling.

Ned stands and reaches into the pocket of his khakis. He pulls out some crumpled papers and begins unfolding them. I can see they are crinkled and worn as he smoothes them out.

"Maybe these will help explain it," he says, handing me the three pieces of well-worn stationery. As I take them, I realize there's something familiar about the paper. *Could it be?* In the upper lefthand corner of each wrinkled sheet is a butterfly! *A butterfly! Where have I seen that before? Beth?* I look closer, trying to make out the faded handwriting. "Dear Ned," the first one says. "As Annie's close friend . . ." *It IS Beth!*

"Beth did this!" I say out loud. "Dear, sweet Beth. *She's* the one who caused us to be apart." I am in shock as I continue reading the letters.

*April 3, 1963*

*Dear Ned, As Annie's close friend, I feel I have to share this with you. She is <u>very</u> unhappy, and I think you are the cause. She spends all her time pining over you, and this keeps her from enjoying her time at MWC. Perhaps if you would encourage her to not build her whole life around you, she would make more of a social life for herself here, and she would be happier. I am worried about her. Thanks.*

*Annie's friend, Beth*

*September 8, 1963*

*Dear Ned, Now that Annie and I are roommates, I see every day that she is still suffering. She even said she wished she were dead! I am very worried about her. I talked to her parents, and they are worried too, and they don't know what to do. I think you need to be more explicit in telling her to go out with others.*
*Thank you.*

*Beth*

*November 2, 1963*

*Dear Ned, You need to stop leading Annie on—as long as you keep writing to her, she won't go out with anyone else. You need to tell her it's over and stop writing to her. She is really miserable. If you care about her, you need to do this for her.*

*Beth*

I am furious! "*She* kept us apart!" I say again, still in shock. "This is too sad for words," I tell him, crying.

"I wonder why she did that," Ned says. "Wasn't she your friend? Maybe she was really concerned about you, like she said."

"Well, I thought so," I say, remembering back. "And then she was my in-law. She was Frank's cousin. She introduced us. Maybe she just wanted me to be part of her family, so she manipulated us to make it happen, for her own selfish reasons. So hard to believe . . .," I say, lost in thought about the past—how she arranged our dates, implemented our engagement, planned our wedding. And writing these notes telling Ned to break up with me! "I never even saw it happening . . ."

"Are you going to confront her about it now?" Ned asks. "Is she still around?"

"No, she isn't," I tell him. "She died in 1991. I will never have closure with her." I am crying again.

Ned comes over and sits next to me on the couch and puts an arm around me. I put my head on his shoulder. He puts his other arm around me, holding me close. He is crying too. He pulls back and looks at me.

"I love you so much, Annie. I've always loved you," he whispers.

I try to stop crying. "Don't say that," I say.

He holds me tight. It feels so good to be in his arms. *I know this is where I belong. It's where I should have been all these years.*

"It's true," Ned says. "I never stopped loving you."

"How can that be?" I ask finally. "You were married to someone else. Didn't you love her?"

"I thought I did," he replies. "But she apparently thought otherwise. She divorced me."

"Why did she do that?" I am really curious, not being able to imagine ever wanting to divorce Ned, if I were ever married to him, that is.

"Because I kept saying 'Annie' in my sleep," he says.

"Seriously?" I question.

"Well, *I* never heard me," he says, "but she claims I did it a number of times. She wasn't too pleased about it."

"So she divorced you for something you said in your sleep?" I ask.

"Yes, well, indirectly," he says. "The last time it happened, a couple of years ago, she started questioning me about you. I told her the truth. I didn't see any point in lying."

"And what *was* the truth?" I ask him.

"It's what I told you," he says. "That I had to break up with you because I was making you miserable. It wasn't because I wanted to or because I didn't love you. It was because I loved you so much," he says.

"It sounds like a tragic love story," I say.

"It *is* a tragic love story," Ned says. "And Dorothy thought so too. Especially when I started saying your name in my sleep."

"Do you think you loved me all that time?" I ask him.

"Here's what I think," he responds without hesitation. "I think my love was like an ember that continued to burn. It never went out but was always glowing beneath the surface. The minute I saw you again, when you opened that door a little while ago and were standing there in all your beauty, that ember flared up and let me know, without a doubt, that nothing has changed. I love you as much now as I did when we were eighteen. Or maybe more."

We sit quietly. I am trying to take it all in. *Is this a dream?* I wonder. *No, this is the awakening from a bad dream.*

"Annie," he says, almost in a whisper, "I've told you my feelings. How do *you* feel?"

"I feel sad," I say, "thinking about what could have been."

"We can't go there," Ned admonishes. "We can't change what happened. All we can do is make up for lost time." He pulls back and looks at me again. "Do you think you could love me again?" he asks.

"Oh, Ned, I think I *do* love you. What you said about the ember thing, I feel that way too. The minute I saw you, I knew. All the feelings came rushing back."

Our bodies are drawn together like magnets. His lips are on mine, pressing hard. I lose myself in the kissing. *What is that feeling? Oh my god. It's the tingling!* I start to cry again.

"What is it now?" he asks, looking at me.

"It's just, uh, I haven't felt this way in, what, forty-seven years? I feel like a teenager again! I didn't even know I could still have these feelings! Your touch sends little electric pulses all through my body, causing my senses to come alive, just like it used to! It's like my body is waking from a coma."

"I'm glad," he says. "You do that to me too. But what about all those years you were married? Didn't you feel that way with him, at least at first?"

"Um, not exactly. Frank was not as sensual . . . I mean, uh, he was nice enough, and I know he loved me and all, but well, sex just wasn't that important to him. He was not a passionate person. Or maybe he just wasn't *you*, as Ringo always liked to point out . . ."

# CHAPTER 48

## "If I Could Turn Back Time"[48]

I stand up and take Ned's hands and pull him up too, then lead him into the bedroom. I sit him on the bed and remove his shoes.

"Let's just lie here and hold each other," I say. "And never let go. But first, let me do this," I add, turning towards the dresser and lighting the green candle.

We lie on the bed in a tight embrace. Ned is rubbing my back and my shoulders.

"I need to make it up to you," he says. He kisses my head and my neck. Nerve endings are coming alive and bursting everywhere he touches. *This feels so familiar, so right.* He kisses my belly and my thighs. *Where did my clothes go?*

He is there, between my legs. I feel the softness of his tongue, and I can't help myself. I am groaning loudly as I burst into orgasm! He does it again. And again.

I reach down and discover his clothes are off as well. He gets on top of me. Our bodies are as one as he gently seeks penetration.

"It still feels like an egg," I say, remembering our first time. He chuckles.

We begin moving in perfect harmony, each acutely aware of the other's pleasure as we explode together.

---

48. "If I Could Turn Back Time"; artist: Cher; released 1989.

"If this is a dream, don't wake me," I say.

"This is not a dream, Annie," he says, carefully rolling off me and pulling the sheet up over us. "This is real." We quietly hold each other. "This is what I'm thinking," Ned says. "I think our souls have always been together. I mean *always*, since the beginning of time, and all those years that we were apart. And that they always will be. And for this brief moment in time, our bodies are together too."

"I like the 'bodies together' part," I say, smiling. "I never want to be apart ever again."

He props himself up on one elbow, looking at me with those green eyes and with a hint of a smile. "You will always be a goddess to me," he says softly, wrapping me in his arms, encompassing my whole being. I allow myself to luxuriate in the moment. *This* moment. I have lived my whole life for *this* moment.

We drift off to sleep, locked in an embrace, as close together as two beings can be.

I awake early, just after five o'clock, looking over to make sure yesterday's astonishing developments weren't all in my imagination. He is there, stirring now and opening one eye.

"Good morning, Beautiful," he says. I don't feel beautiful, but I smile at his words.

"Why don't we go shower?" I say. He nods in agreement.

As I get up to start the water, I hear a ping on my phone, which is lying on the dresser, next to the burned-out candle. I check to see who is texting so early in the morning. It's Ringo.

> *"I can't stand it any longer. How did it go with Ned? What happened?"*

Not wanting to take the time for a lengthy reply, I simply send her back a smiley face emoji. *She'll figure it out,* I muse.

Ned joins me for a leisurely shower, something we've never done before, the leisurely part, that is. That one time we did shower together was the morning from hell, when he was leaving for Vietnam. A lifetime ago.

"I don't even know if you like coffee in the morning," I tell him as he's patting down my dripping body with one of the newly laundered towels I put out yesterday.

"Oh yes. I'm an avid coffee drinker," he replies. "How about you?"

"Yes, me too."

"Glad to know we have the important things in common," he quips.

After getting dressed, I make eggs and toast, along with coffee, for the two of us, and we sit at my kitchen table, eating breakfast just like an old married couple.

"I think Tulip approves of you," I tell him. "She slept on the floor by the foot of our bed all night." *Did he catch that I said "our" bed?*

"Maybe she knows this is her family now," Ned replies, reaching down to pat Tulip, who is waiting patiently by the table for any morsels that might fall her way.

"Is it, Ned? Are we your family now?" I ask.

"I hope so, Annie," he says. "I don't want to spend another minute away from you."

"It's not that simple," I say. "I have kids and grandkids. So do you. Don't we have to let them know first? Get their approval or something? And I live here. You live in Colorado, two thousand miles away."

"I will move anywhere to be with you, even to the moon if necessary," Ned replies, taking my hand. "And how could our families *not* approve when they see how happy we are?"

I marvel at how normal it feels, sitting here with Ned, discussing our future over the breakfast table. *How easy it would be to have him just move into my life. Shouldn't I at least have a little guilt, being so happy here with Ned in what used to be Frank's and my special place? No! I deserve to be happy! Ned and I must make up for lost time. No point in second guessing now.*

"And then we'll get married, right?" Ned continues. "Our families will meet and all give their blessings, and then we'll have the wedding you always talked about—bridesmaids, a church, and all our friends, along with our children and grandchildren!"

As I'm contemplating that thought, I get up and start clearing the breakfast dishes. Standing at the sink, I feel his arms gently encircling my waist, and soft kisses on the back of my neck.

"I could get used to this," I mumble between shivers.

"I hope you do," Ned replies. Then he adds, "How about we go back to bed for a little morning 'nap'? The dishes can wait."

I readily agree.

\*\*\*

Over dinner, we catch up on our families. Ned tells me that his mother died shortly after the move to Arizona, over forty years ago. His father, however, lived for another twenty years, meeting a lovely woman, to whom he was happily married for nearly fifteen years. "I was pleased he was able to find happiness again and make a new life for himself," Ned adds.

"How about your parents? Either of them still around?" he asks. I explain that my parents both passed eight years ago, within a few months of each other. "It was quite fitting, and comforting to me," I explain. "Neither of them had much of a social life, and they depended so much on each other. Either of them alone would have been lost."

Then Ned changes the subject. "I'll be leaving in the morning," he announces calmly.

"What? Just like that? You're walking out of my life, *again*?" I reply, somewhat startled.

"Oh, but I'll be back, and this time I mean it," he says. "I have a dentist appointment on Thursday, then some important business to attend to, like putting my house on the market and telling my kids and grandkids about us. I'll be back next week, okay? That will give you this weekend to give your family all the details as well."

"Um, I don't think I'll give them *all* the details," I reply, "but okay, that sounds perfect. I suppose I can manage one more goodbye with you, but never again after tomorrow."

"I promise," he says. "No more goodbyes. Ever. I love you so much."

"I love you too," I say.

# EPILOGUE—FUTURE PERFECT

Ned and Annie have a late summer wedding, the big ceremony she's always dreamed of with a white dress and bridesmaids. Her grandson, little Joey, gives her away.

The following spring, they make a trip back to where it all began, their little hometown of Fort Custis, to attend their fiftieth high school reunion.

# ABOUT THE AUTHOR

Ginny Brinkley, a native of Virginia, is a graduate of Washington-Lee High School in Arlington, Virginia; Mary Washington College (now the University of Mary Washington) in Fredericksburg, Virginia; and the University of North Florida in Jacksonville, Florida, where she received a masters of business administration.

Ginny began writing at a young age, composing stories about her dog, Dusty, and her cat, Purr Purr, and illustrating them with black and white photos taken with her Brownie Hawkeye camera. Her writing developed into a career when she co-authored a best-selling manual on pregnancy and childbirth, *Your Child's First Journey*, published in 1981 (Avery Publishing Group), and later revised as *Pregnancy to Parenthood* (Penguin Putnam).

In 1989, she co-founded Pink Inc! Publishing, producer of educational materials for pregnant and parenting teens. Among the books she co-authored during this time were *Young and Pregnant, You and Your New Baby, Baby and Me, What's Right for Me?* and *"You're WHAT?"*

No longer in the publishing business after selling Pink Inc! in 2001, Ginny joined a weekly writing group and changed her focus to fiction. Her first novel, *EarthQuest—A story of life, love and the pursuit of red meat*, was published in 2011 (available at belleairepress.com). This intriguing sci-fi tale was co-authored by fellow Star Writing Group member, Kathleen Perry.

Ginny lives on a lake in Hawthorne, Florida, with her husband, Bill, of forty years. They have five grown children and a total of fifteen grandchildren. Besides writing, Ginny enjoys water skiing, jet skiing, stand-up paddle boarding, and, when time and family commitments permit, spending time in Maui.